THE BOOKSTORE

Dianne Kochenburg

This book is dedicated to my amazing daughters, Karen and Sheri...and to Mea and Murphy, my ever-present writing companions and aspiring bookstore cats.

CONTENTS

CHAPTER 1

The fog horns reminded Alex that she now lived in a Beach town. Seaside, Oregon. She felt the oppressive weather in her bones. The bedside clock read 5:15 am. Time to get up. The cats were eager for the morning to begin. Their food bowl was empty. She slid out of bed and found her ratty slippers. Her robe was nearby. It was cold in her aging beach cottage.

Her house had been a bargain, just under her budget of half a million. It was a short drive or a long walk to Broadway, where she and her business partner's bookstore was located. Luckily, the furnace worked. Her little place would be warm within minutes. That helped her to cope with the continual dampness, the faint moldy smell, the persistent fog and rain, and the biting cold Oregon wind.

Alex was from the California Bay Area, where the sun shines relentlessly. She was another early retiree from the tech industry who wanted to escape. She'd been an Oregon resident for about six weeks now. Not enough time to feel like she was home.

Oregon gets more than its share of us, she thought. She paid cash for the house, so there were no mortgage payments to worry about. Her neighbors, on the other hand, who mostly worked in the service industry, were struggling with their mortgages and the big grocery bills these days. One of the many reasons Oregonians resented California retirees.

The post-pandemic world was different. Everybody was still a little shell-shocked. Lots of folks were on the move, fuck it, do your dream. Alex wanted to live her romantic fantasy of going into the book business. So did her workmate, best buddy, and now business partner, Darlene.

It had been Darlene's idea to cash out, move to Oregon, and open a bookstore. Take life easy. She said Seaside was the place. An hour and a half or so from Portland. Oregonians love bookstores, coffee houses, brew pubs, and the beach, even in the winter. They convinced each other that they had to escape to Oregon.

They found the perfect location for the store on the outskirts of town, on Broadway, where several renovated buildings were awaiting new tenants. A Starbucks and a cafe were close by.

The vacant ex-clothing store was what attracted Alex and Darlene. The building was hollowed-out, polished up and waiting for them. It had beautiful Victorian doors with beveled glass panels framed in polished mahogany, and inviting display windows on either side. Tilework and brick showcased the storefront. One look and they knew it would be their perfect venue.

The store had a loft apartment above it, which became Darlene's home. She was the owner above the bookstore, an old-fashioned but practical idea.

Alex padded out to the kitchen and fed the cats who were winding around her legs as she opened the picky-eater cat food that they loved. The kitchen's last update had been years ago, but it was clean and freshly painted. The old appliances were okay because Alex didn't cook that much. Somebody had probably raised a family in the kitchen. The chrome table and four chairs were worn, attesting to that fact. It was comforting to think that a happy family had lived there.

She made herself a coffee and sat down with her iPad to look at her chore list and then check email and Facebook before starting her day. Ah yes, it was Monday, book scout day. She would drive to Portland, the Beaverton area, and check out the toniest of Goodwills for bargains on quality used books. Then she would make the rounds of several Dollar Stores for new books. The dregs of the remainders went there. Occasionally she'd find some romance novels or mysteries with great-looking covers. Eye candy for browsers in their store.

By the time Alex had breakfast, did the household chores, played with the cats, and rechecked the incoming email, it was time for a shower. One quick look in Alex's small closet revealed that she was not too interested in clothes. Hers was a no-nonsense wardrobe of what seemed appropriate for her new job, her version of bookstore-owner clothes.

Today she'd wear sweats for driving, plus a long-sleeved tee shirt and a jean jacket. In and out of stores, buying used books, and stashing them in her car was work. Scrambling through thrift shops was a dirty job.

Alex was a tall, brown-haired, average-looking, middle-aged woman. She tried to keep her weight down, a tough battle. She wore glasses and no makeup. A leftover from Covid and working from home. Who the hell cares anymore? Nobody would notice her. It was not like she had friends in town.

She texted Darlene to tell her she was leaving and took off in her gray Subaru Forester. It was a good choice for Oregon roads, lots of room for books with the back seats down. By 8:30 the commuters were ahead of her. The roads were still slick with rain, but drivable. She'd be heading over the coast range, so it would be hilly driving over decent roads. Lots of trees. Douglas Fir, the dark, menacing rainforest of coastal Oregon. It took her about two hours to make the trip. She cruised into Beaverton and checked her phone. Yup. She remembered. There were three Goodwills, fairly close together.

Owning a bookstore was a labor of love. Independents were in serious jeopardy these days. Probably very few were opening, in fact, most were closing. Electronic readers, ebooks, and audibles were the thing. Amazon for book purchases. Who needs to visit a real bookstore these days? Order it and have it at your door the next day.

But bookstores still appealed to a lot of people. They were where customers went to buy books the old fashioned way. There is something about walking into a bookstore. Buildings that store knowledge. Romance, intrigue, mysteries, history and a wealth of knowledge all reside there.

For the bookstore owner, it was always about the stock, finding the right books, displaying them, shelving them and helping a buyer find the last store copy. Crowding too many books into a store overwhelms the customers, and empty shelves disappoint them.

Alex and Darlene decided from the beginning that they would sell both new and gently-used, second-hand books. It was a cost-cutting measure. There were a lot of shelves to fill. Used books were prolific. They could buy them cheaply, clean them up, and sell them again.

They would purchase new best sellers to draw in customers, hoping that their wide array of older, wiser books of an uncertain age would flirt with them from the shelves of newly established Seaside Bookstore.

Knowing the stock was the thing. Alex purchased small hand scanners that linked up with their electronic inventory system. When a book comes in, scan its ISBN, and it's in the system, complete with lots of other information.

Choose the right books and then sell the little darlings. Get the money. The whole purpose. In the meantime, you have to become aware of the books themselves, their private lives. Buyers will sometimes quiz you. Don't try to fake it. If you don't know the book, listen, they will tell you maybe more than you want to know.

When you hunt for good used books, always be on the lookout for the classics that other book scouts might have missed. And always buy Stephen King, John Grisham, Janet Evanovitch and Reacher. Consider Moby Dick, Agatha Christie and Sherlock Holmes. Occasionally, if you are lucky, somebody's whole library gets dumped by the kids when the time comes. It will be evident, if you know what you are looking at. A home library is a treasure trove. Mondays are good days to spot them.

None of the Goodwills Alex searched this morning had many great deals, so onto the Dollar Stores. Some of these gamey-smelling cheap-junk bargain stores treat their books well, while others abuse them on the shelves. Alex found possibilities at several stores. She was looking for attractive book covers. The jury had already decided that the Dollar Store books were losers. But twenty bucks for twenty new pretty faces was not so bad for shills.

While Alex was in town, she hit a few other thrifts. Salvation Army carried books too. She picked up a dozen or so from them, nothing outstanding, just good used books that needed a new home. Selling used books was their bread and butter, and scouting was the cheapest way to restock. She had cardboard boxes in her car so she'd know how well she was doing by how many boxes were filled. Thirty books per box equaled one shelf.

She stopped for a quick lunch, then hit Hillsborough on the way back to Seaside. Not a bad haul there. Her purchases weren't limited to fiction. There were lots of non-fiction selections that needed a new home, like cookbooks, DIY of any kind, history books, art books, nature, memoir and biography.

The thing about thrift stores was that they sold all their books for one price. Usually $1.49 for hardbacks and $.50 for all types of softbacks. Thrift stores were disdainful of books. Troublesome space-wasters. Seaside Books cleaned them up and priced them for what they were actually worth, a labor-intensive time-consuming job.

Alex was thinking of a typical Silicon Valley Monday morning at her laptop, working remotely and getting mentally ready for whatever fresh hell was coming along next. Zoom meetings, email frenzies, project manager reports, pep talks, and annoying overachievers sucking up all the air and optimism. Monday's new resolve headed out the window as soon as the coffee went cold.

Driving around looking for used books was better for her mental health, but, unfortunately, running a small retail business was no kind of a money maker. Good thing she and Darlene had savings. It probably would be a long slog before they started to break even.

Alex was back at the bookstore by four. Mondays were 'sorry, we're closed' days. They both worked anyhow. Restocking and refreshing their windows. Their store was in a foot-traffic area, so refreshing windows, cleaning, dusting, and polishing were all part of the game.

Alex and Dar would tackle the used books together. All stickers peeled off, and jackets or covers all wiped clean with alcohol. Check for things left in books. Always fun. Also, check editions and autographs. Signed books got their own shelf. So did some firsts. Genres were separated for shelving, and all books needed scanning. Getting used books ready to go on the shelves was a big job. They might work into the night and have to grab burgers at midnight and keep going.

They opened for business on Tuesdays at ten and stayed open until 7 pm or 10 depending on the time of year. They split the shifts. Their one male employee worked Friday, Saturday, and Sunday with them. He was young and knowledgeable, a book geek, a heavy lifter, and good with people. His name was Ethan Patel. Indian, nearly twenty, a full-time college student at Clatsop Community College, working on a liberal arts degree at the moment, even though his folks still thought he was going to be a scientist.

Seaside was not some crime-ridden slum, but it did have a few problems with the petty stuff. However, most hoodlums veer toward the gas stations and 7-11s. Bookstores were not known for big spending or tills full of cash, nothing edible, drinkable, or smokable in sight. Nothing pawnable. So the store had only a slight risk of burglary.

Nevertheless, they installed cameras, alarms, double locks, and shatterproof windows. And they hired Ethan. When things were slow, he read or studied. He was on deck and prominent when things were busy.

Neither of them wanted to talk about the financial situation. Ethan was one of their bigger overhead costs. They paid him twelve bucks an hour and never supervised his time. Neither Darlene nor Alex got a salary. They did get reimbursed for money they spent out of pocket. They owned the building outright.

Darlene's loft was an adequate space, clean and cozy, with an updated kitchen and bath. She was happy to be there. Her outside stairs were locked and alarmed. They took all the precautions they could. The local cops patrolled often.

They wouldn't consider themselves profitable until they received paychecks. The weekends were their busy time, and weekdays were slow. Five hundred-dollar days were worth celebrating. They rarely happened. They weren't coming close to getting paid. Every extra dollar went back into the store. There was so much they needed to learn about the business.

On Tuesday mornings they were always both on hand to open. The front counter and cash register overlooked the table displays, the door, and the front windows. One of them tried to be close to the desk, as they called it, at all times. Darlene took the mornings, and Alex took over when she had lunch.

Most sales were credit cards, but a few were cash. Nobody offered to write a check. Customers liked to talk, so the pace of making the sale was slow. If customers began lining up, they both worked the desk.

Occasionally, an older person might ask them to order a book. They ordered them through Amazon and had them delivered to the customer for a five-dollar fee. The older customers were always grateful because it was frustrating not to get a book they wanted because they lacked the computer skills.

They spent long days on their feet, so they were happy to hit the stools behind the desk when the time came. It was a surprise just how much work there was behind the scenes. The two of them were trying to do it all, with Ethan as backup.

They did have a back room for receiving new books. The delivery folks brought the boxes in on their dollies and took them straight to the back. The boxes usually remained unopened until Ethan came in. He muscled them open, scanned them into the system, and stacked the books onto rolling carts for shelving.

When Alex showed up Tuesday morning, Darlene was anxious to see her.

"Alex! Guess what I finally worked on?"

Alex smiled. It could be anything on their huge to-do list. "Let's see, our automatic Doordash delivery?"

"Noooooo, our website!" she said triumphantly.

"Oh? Wow! That's great. Let's take a look. I can't believe you found the time or energy for it."

Darlene pushed her laptop across the counter. There it was, The Seaside Bookstore's website, complete with interior photos, including the charming old-fashioned entrance and beautifully restored Victorian doors with their name in foot-high gold-leaf lettering.

The site featured the two big book events that began each new year: Black History and banned books. The feature table was draped in crime scene tape for a little humor. Unfortunately, this was a touchy year to joke about banned books. Other photos included the annual sale table of books they were clearing out for inventory purposes. Since they were a newly opened store, close-out sales were tongue-in-cheek. It wasn't too soon to preview Valentine's Day.

"It's beautiful, Dar. Your talent always boggles my mind. We have such an advantage with your work experience. Most businesses can't afford you."

"Ah, thanks. It's fun and exciting to be building our own website after all these years of doing it for others. Anyhow, I spent most of yesterday and half the night on it. If you approve, I'll go ahead and launch it."

"Sure thing, let's go for it."

Darlene added, "I also pulled together our customer email list. We have quite a few entries, including all the other folks we want to work with. We should expect some traffic from this first announcement. And I'm hoping we get a few requests for book signing sessions from local authors soon. Fingers crossed, right? And I'll add online sales soon. We have to decide which books to sell that way. A decision for our next strategy meeting."

"Right, and we gotta start making money. We need a few more employees. A bookkeeper, for example," Alex said, thinking out loud.

"And marketing."

They both nodded.

It was another slow day, so Alex worked on bookkeeper duties. She paid bills, caught up on

Ethan's pay deductions, and recorded the gross income for the past week, which was pathetic. They were working like mad, nearly every day, long hours, trying to think positively. She looked back on the two previous months' income. It was inching up ever so slowly. How on earth did other booksellers do it?

Sell more books, sell at higher prices. That's all they had unless they could come up with another idea. What else is there to sell? Book related? Vendors had already pedaled lots of stuff to them, all too expensive wholesale. The greeting card ladies had been in. Cards sell well but are costly to buy wholesale. Hmm.

Alex called Darlene over to the desk, where she was looking at the catalogs and info on peripherals that they could sell at the cash register. She liked chocolate. Maybe they could talk to the candy vendors again. Darlene agreed.

Alex continued, "Dar, could you design some simple greeting cards we could sell at the cash register?"

"Maybe. We're that desperate?" Darlene was skeptical.

"Well, here's what I'm thinking. Everybody else does it, so it must be worth it. If we can offer handmade greeting cards, maybe it will help." Alex was scanning the card brochures. "Look at these."

Darlene looked them over carefully. "Oh, hmm. I'll check Pinterest for some ideas. And I'll make a run to Michaels. See what I can come up with."

They closed up that night. Darlene went to her loft, and Alex drove the mile to her little cottage. They were both exhausted. They had both made six-figure salaries at their tech jobs. Now they were literally pinching pennies and taking no salaries to make this business work. The long hours were killing them.

The cats were in the window waiting for Alex. She felt sorry for them being home alone all the time. They were used to her always being there. She was tired, so she fixed a quick dinner, held some play time, and then went off to bed. She read personal emails and Facebook posts until she was too sleepy to think any longer. She missed having friends.

Darlene was alone in her loft. It was warm. She had a combined kitchen and family room, and a bed and bath in the back, away from the road noise. She would be too tired to notice any noise tonight. After a quick grilled cheese sandwich, she sat at the table, flipping through Pinterest on greeting cards. So many to choose from. And bookmarks, yes. Even easier. Large postal tags, with twine through the hole in the top. She would check Michaels tomorrow to see if she could make them at a profit. Cards were expensive these days.

She laughed. She could sell her creative services online from home and make thousands. Yet she would earn a handful of dollars doing handmade greeting cards. Ah, well, it's a retirement pastime now. And it's supposed to be fun. Remember that.

CHAPTER 2

The following Monday was Darlene's turn to be the book scout. She decided to try the Troutdale area. Thrift stores and Dollar Stores again. They ignored second-hand bookstores. They were too savvy about prices. Estate sales were good sources for inventory, but other book scouts would be fighting over the books too. And if it was a managed estate sale, invited booksellers and appraisers would have bought up the good stuff in the preview sale.

Darlene was short, petite, and freckled. All disadvantages in negotiations. Her reddish hair, glasses, and tastefully drab wardrobe disguised her talent and brain power. She had learned to use those disadvantages rather than letting them work against her. She looked like any housewife as she browsed the Goodwill, pushing the big cart around, looking confused at times.

The Troutdale Goodwill was bustling, and the workers were busy restocking shelves. The bookshelves were groaning, and the workers had problems finding shelf space for all the books. They were stacking them in piles on the shelves.

Darlene figured she might have hit a large, dumped collection. The workers used wheeled canvas carts to get stuff out onto the floor. One cart was sitting there abandoned in an aisle while the workers fought to get the first cart unloaded.

She spotted a handful of old books without book jackets on them. They looked to be in good shape. Darlene reached in, grabbed them, and dropped them into the bottom of her cart. They were really old, written in another language. She got a few more before the workers pulled the cart up to the bookshelves.

She started browsing the books already shelved. The workers were giving her dirty looks because she was in the way. She ignored them and started loading books into her cart, mostly classics, all in good shape. Then she decided to check out before somebody got too suspicious. The Goodwill hates it when they miss a treasure in the junk.

So Darlene paid the usual $1.49 in cash for each hardback and ran them out to her Honda with the empty boxes waiting for the be filled. She would make one more run into the store for another load. Another obvious scout was there by then, talking, no arguing, with the workers. He wanted to buy the lot. Rats. Darlene managed to snag a few more books before the manager came out to referee. She hit the checkout and ran to her car with her possible deal of the day.

Then on to the Dollar Store. They sell candy at the register. She noticed Godiva bars for a dollar each. And boxes of them stacked up too. She asked if she could buy them by the boxful. She smiled shyly. She loved Godiva. They settled on a price. She walked away with 96 bars that they could probably sell for 2.50 each. She had paid less than a dollar each for them.

She couldn't wait to get the books home. Maybe there would be a pleasant surprise. At least the candy would be a winner.

Alex helped her unload them. They stacked the books on the large table in the back and sorted them into genres. Most were classics, and some might have value. They would do internet research on them. It might make a good project for Ethan. He didn't know it yet, but they were training him for the assistant manager's job when they became successful enough to hire employees. These books might be the first candidates for their online store.

The next morning the old books were sitting in a pile by themselves, yet to be dealt with. Darlene riffed through the pages and gasped. "Alex, look at this!"

"Holy crap!" Alex exclaimed, illustrated Latin books, beautiful, very old. She handled them carefully. "I think you hit a gold mine. What do we do with these?"

"Hmm. An auction house, maybe. Rare book dealer?" Darlene was taking a closer look. "Wow! Check this out."

Darlene showed Alex a book that was all handwritten, with beautiful calligraphy. Amazing.

Alex pulled out her phone and started looking up rare book dealers in the area. Not many. Lots of ads. Confusing. "Oh, listen to this."

It was a book appraiser-dealer in Cannon Beach. She phoned him. He could see her this morning. Alex thought Darlene should go too.

Alex said, "Let's put up a sign, 'open at 1', and we can both go. If he makes us an offer, I want your okay."

Darlene agreed, but Alex had to do the talking. They packed the books into a tote, with paper around each one. There were five of them altogether.

Cannon Beach wasn't far. They stopped off for a coffee break to kill some time. A roadside place near Haystack Rock. The fog had lifted, but gray skies were everywhere. The rock looked massive this close. The coffee was good, and the pastries were delicious. They were giggling, wondering what was coming next. So much to learn about the book business.

The appraiser was also a pawnbroker. Okay. Interesting. He buzzed them in. A guard sat at the door. Regular business hours hadn't started yet. When the dealer saw who had come through the door, he nodded, and they were led to a desk with chairs for them. The guy introduced himself.

Darlene and Alex were gawking at all the merchandise that was on display. They had no idea how pawnshops operated. He appeared to be amused. After introductions, he asked, "What can I do for you?"

Alex pulled out the books and placed them on the desk. His eyebrows lifted. He carefully picked up one of the books. He put on gloves and turned the pages, examining each book. He looked at the spines and used a special glass to check out the paper. He checked the bindings. He did a comprehensive and thorough inspection of each book.

"Oh, Jeez, where did you get these books?" he finally asked.

Alex said, "Why do I have to reveal that?"

"I need to be assured that they weren't stolen."

Darlene spoke up. "I bought them at the Goodwill yesterday. They were part of a big collection of books they were unloading onto their shelves. I bought quite a few books. These were among them."

He looked at the books for a long time. "Do you have a receipt? Do you have other books like these?"

Darlene opened her purse and pulled up a long receipt. Each line on it read 'book 1.49'. She handed it to him.

He smiled, looked it over, and handed it back and shook his head. He paused, "And you two are the owners of that new bookstore in Seaside. I've heard of it."

They nodded.

"I'll give you five hundred for the lot. That's a huge profit for Goodwill books that you bought for a dollar forty-nine each."

"What are these books really worth?" Alex asked.

"What the buyer is willing to give you. Do you have any other potential buyers in mind?" He smiled like a crocodile.

"There's an appraiser in Portland…"

"Okay," he interrupted, "I'll make it a thousand."

Alex looked at Darlene. She shook her head.

He looked at them again and sighed. He scratched his scaly skin and wiped his forehead with his handkerchief. Took a deep breath.

Was all that just an act? Alex thought. Or were his greed glands working overtime?

"Look, I'd really like to have these books. If you took them to auction, it's a crap shoot. You might get four hundred or four thousand. Even if you got the big number, you have to give the auction house half. You'd be taking a chance. I might have a buyer. I need to make some money too. You'll be making a huge profit.

"Here's my final offer. I'll give you twenty-five hundred for them. Not a penny more. Cash."

Alex looked at Darlene. She didn't crack a smile. She just nodded her head slightly.

"Okay. We'll take it."

"I'll write you a receipt."

He did just that. And counted out twenty-five hundred dollar bills and pushed the pile across the table with his store receipt. "Thank you for coming in today."

He grabbed up the books in his claw-like paws. They didn't shake hands. Alex took the cash and stuffed it into the tote. They were ushered out the front door by the guard. They made it out to the car before breaking into laughter. Tears were running down Darlene's cheeks.

"Holy cow, that was fun," she said. "Now we

know where the money is, rare books we can't even read."

More laughter and head shaking. What a lesson.

"He was sort of creepy, huh?" Alex said. "Have you ever watched Pawn Stars on tv? That whole deal was just like the show. I swear to god."

Dar shook her head. "Do you think he took us for a ride?" she asked.

"Maybe, but he was sweating too much. I think he was pushing it a little. My guess is he'll make some money. I think we did good."

"Ya know, I might have taken the first offer. Even five hundred is a big score for books we paid a dollar forty-nine for."

"Right?"

They spent the afternoon making greeting cards and bookmarks between customers. When they got hungry, they ordered crab salads via Doordash. To celebrate. They talked about the cash. The pawnbroker had given them a receipt. That meant the purchase would be on his books, so they figured the sale should be recorded in their records too. It was tempting to just each pocket half each and not report it. But why take a chance? Their big sale. So the transaction went on the books, and the cash got deposited into their business account.

By the end of the weekend, they had seen a lot of customers. Their first attempt at marketing was paying off. They sold all the bookmarks and most of the greeting cards. The basket of Godiva bars, in the cute basket by the cash register with the sign reading '2.50 each', was nearly empty.

Alex said, "I can't wait to tally our sales tomorrow."

They both knew that finding rare books was maybe a once-in-a-lifetime thing, like the scavenger with the metal detector at the beach. He mostly found soda cans and loose change. But you never know. And once you strike something big, you don't forget it.

But the true significance was that they had a good week. Their first. Reason to hope, and a nice cash balance lifted their spirits. Maybe the bookstore could become successful.

Over the next few months, business began to pick up. As a result, they were able to offer a small selection of magazines, puzzles, word games, and a few newspapers. Items that customers might stop in to pick up often. High-end chocolate bars were also popular.

Darlene created a table of cards, candy, and paperbacks for Valentine's Day, with a selection of gift bags. A last-minute station for customers to put together DIY gifts. It was such a hit that she kept the table stocked all the time. It was a unique gimmick.

Alex reported that their weekly numbers were improving. They were averaging at least one five hundred dollar day per week. Baby steps. They needed five hundred every day.

Increasing their stock was a never-ending chore. They started buying used books three days per week from independent book scouts. The scouts began showing up regularly. Darlene and Alex suspended their long distance scouting for a while. Instead they looked at the bags and boxes that came through the doors. It was also time-consuming, but they didn't have to make the long drives to get more stock. The trade-off, of course, was there was only a slim chance of seeing a rare book come in off the street.

Their store was a long rectangle with a high ceiling. The back of it wasn't used as much. So they decided to do something to bring it to the customers' attention. They brought in the contractor and told him their idea. They wanted the floor raised in the back, like a stage, so that it was noticeable from the front. With a few steps up to it, and railings on each side.

The stage could be used for meetings or author visits. They'd wire it for sound and maybe add a projector for special events. Chairs and a podium could be set up easily. Maybe they could bring in a designer to smarten it up. The contractor went to work. It wasn't a difficult job.

They invited local writers in to read and sign books. Book clubs might want to hold their book-choosing meetings at the store. For a small fee, they would provide a facilitator to help them.

One day a couple came into the store with a question for them. Darlene recognized them. They came in often. They were wondering if they could use the lovely spot at the back of the store for a small wedding?

Darlene called Alex over. They both listened to the idea. The couple would invite maybe twenty guests. They'd bring in a preacher to officiate. Then they would host a very simple reception, with cake and champagne. Little mess or clean up required. The kicker was they would ask their guests to buy them books instead of traditional wedding gifts.

Darlene and Alex looked at each other and nodded, grinning. What a great idea. They loved it. They worked out the details. It would be after hours, so room prep, and clean up would be needed, and both owners and Ethan would be on hand to assist. So they would charge the couple $500 for the overhead costs. If that seemed reasonable, choose a date. They did.

The couple left the store in a good mood. Their

idea for a unique wedding had been accepted. It would be a very inexpensive affair, and they would receive gifts that they could actually use. The cost of the reception was within their budget. Neither of them wanted a traditional wedding. All the expense and planning was not something they wanted to do. Both of their parents promised them large checks if they would agree to a small wedding.

Three weeks later, the wedding took place. Ethan did the set up. He would play host for the store and make things run smoothly. He would earn $200 and would be affectionately known as the wedding planner. All three of them dressed for the occasion. Ethan wore a black suit with a blue shirt. Darlene and Alex decided blue was their color too. A tradition was born.

Ethan helped the couple with background music, an iPhone playlist and speakers. It worked just fine. A mic for the preacher was provided. Folding chairs were arranged. A festive table for dessert and champagne was readied. A complimentary bouquet from the store adorned the table. Everything was perfect for the guests' arrival.

The store had been shined up and aglow for the big event. A special book display provided suggestions for the happy couple should the guests need help choosing just the right book.

Ethan's little sister showed up to be the gift wrap girl. What a great idea. She would receive a jar full of tips, an unexpected, but very nice gesture.

The evening went off brilliantly. The preacher was a hip guy with a sense of humor. The music played softly as the bride and groom showed up in their best, wide-eyed and smiling. Their parents and the guests seemed happy and excited to be invited to such a unique wedding.

The reception was so easy. The couple opted for gorgeous wedding cupcakes on a tiered tray. The champagne flowed in plastic stemware. The noise level rose. The couple was royally cheered. The wedding toasts were hilarious. The reception was soon over. Time for gift buying. Everybody was eager and feeling generous.

They strolled the store and bought everything from coffee table books to recipe books, mysteries, and love stories. Even the humor and finance sections were perused. Several baby books were purchased too by knowing relatives. Little sister was busy, so Darlene helped her lovingly wrap the gifts and place them into bookstore handle bags.

The bags stacked up. The couple received so many books that Ethan brought out boxes for their trip to the car. Everybody had a wonderful time. The guest count went way over twenty. It didn't seem to matter. There was plenty of room, lots of champagne and luckily, extra cupcakes. At the end of the evening, the bride and groom and family formed a reception line at the door for handshakes, fist pumps, five fives, and hugs all around as the happy guests left the store.

Alex, Darlene, and Ethan were giddy when it was over. The wedding had been a brilliant success. Everything worked, no hitches or surprises. The guests behaved themselves, probably because they weren't sitting around captive for hours on end. Preliminary tallies showed sales of over two thousand dollars. Oh my god.

CHAPTER 3

"We've got to talk."

Alex had just walked in. It was Monday, their closed day, the day they met and talked strategy for the week, set their schedules, figured out what was most pressing, and who would bird dog it.

Alex said, "Okay. Since we spend most of Monday talking, I'm guessing you don't mean talk about the bookstore, right?"

Darlene nodded.

Alex sighed. "Remember when we used to talk, like all the time, about personal stuff, and how we were feeling? You've just reminded me. We haven't been doing that lately, huh?"

Darlene agreed, "Nope. You're gonna need coffee first. This is important."

Alex went back to receiving, where their makeshift break room was, and built herself a cup of instant. She noticed that things were in pretty good shape, with a few boxes of books waiting to be scanned and shelved. Gotta love Ethan.

She returned to the front, sat on a stool beside Darlene, and said, "Okay, what's up?"

Darlene took a deep breath and straightened up, "I'm pregnant."

Alex's whole face lit up. "Really? Oh my god! How did that happen? Wow! No kidding?"

Darlene just stared at her. Of all the responses, joy was the last one she thought she'd hear from Alex.

"Right? I just found out. It surprised me too, sort of. I'm not exactly sure how I feel about it. It wasn't entirely unplanned. I've thought for a while that I might want to have a child."

Alex grinned. "So you figured out how to have a social life. Wow. Good for you. I've been so caught up in the store, and I'm so exhausted by the end of the day that having sex hasn't hit my radar screen. And opportunity is nowhere close. So I'm all ears. Who's the guy?"

Darlene was so relieved. She had thought Alex would want to hustle her off to Planned Parenthood the minute she heard the news. It was going to be okay. She shouldn't have worried.

So Darlene quickly told her the story, a familiar tale of lust and loneliness.

"Blame Starbucks. I've been heading over there

most mornings for a latte before work. I'm a regular, like many others. I sit at the same table every morning, check my phone, and read the paper. So this guy, about my age, started to join me. Vacant seat. You know how crowded Starbucks is in the morning."

"Uh-huh. How many couples do we know hooked up in Starbucks?" Alex reminded her.

Darlene sighed. "I know. But I never gave it a thought. Morning Starbucks isn't the same as a Starbucks date, where you decide whether you want to — you know — with someone. I'm just sitting there doing my thing, and so is he. Every morning. Pretty soon, it's good morning and a smile. Then it's have a nice day. Then it's, oh, I missed you yesterday. Then, one morning, he sits down, and we stare at each other for a long time. I can feel my heart beating. And I notice that he's kinda cute in his tight jeans and work boots. His low voice, his polite ways.

"He grins at me and whispers, 'Ya wanna do it? I know that I sure do.' Without blinking, I say yes, How about now?"

I take him upstairs, and we have just about the best sex ever. We're still doing it. He stops at Starbucks and picks up the coffee. We drink, we make love without a care, and then guess what? Oops, I'm pregnant."

"Well, yes," Alex said, "it happens."

Darlene continued, "I know. I'm 41. I think this could be my last chance. So we're together now. Tru's his name, and he's hot and nice too. We will have a pretty baby girl together. Tru's divorced, has kids, money problems, and works construction.

"But I don't care. I'm not going to marry him. I just told him the news this morning. He panicked at first. Then I told him he could consider himself the sperm donor. He was relieved."

"Jeez, Darlene, you are so gutsy. That's quite a story."

"Yup, it is. After all these years, I made a spur-of-the-moment decision that's life-changing. Lately I've been feeling sickish in the morning, so I did the pregnancy test. Positive. You should have seen my hands shake while I was doing it. I was having cold sweats.

"But once I knew for sure, I calmed down. Reality sunk in. I went to the doctor last week. Confirmed it. Everything is good. I'm high risk because of my age, but otherwise, I'm gonna have a baby."

Alex was in tears. "I just love your story. You did it. What a commitment! I'm really proud of you."

"Thanks, Alex, that means everything to me. Oh, and while we're on the subject, let me run this idea by you." Darlene's voice was shaking, like maybe this would be difficult. She was on the edge of tears.

"You know," Alex said, "we're gonna have a million things to figure out, so let's start now. No kidding. I want to help you through this. Whatever you want to talk about, whenever, really."

"Okay, thanks. So I'm into my nesting phase. It's weird. I never pay much attention to where I live. But all of a sudden, this seems so important. I wanna ask you right away."

Alex was puzzled. Nesting? "Sure. Go ahead."

Another deep breath from Darlene. "I wanna switch houses with you. You've got the perfect house for me and a little one. No long set of stairs from the car to the door. The swing set in the backyard, two bedrooms, and the finished basement. It would be perfect for me.

"I even worked out the finances. I'd owe you two hundred thousand. I think you'd love the loft. What do you think? You don't have to answer right away."

"Dar, let me share a secret with you. I've always envied you for getting the loft. You are so right. Of course the cottage would be better for you.

I'd love to live there. I never go out into my yard. Only the gardener does. Same with the basement. The cottage is adorable, but it doesn't suit me at all. So yes, I'd love to switch with you. Whenever you are ready. We can even switch furniture if you want. We can work out the details. We have time."

"Oh my god, Al, thanks. I had no idea that you would have preferred the loft. I guess we need to start talking about stuff that matters again."

They got through the day in fits and starts. Work got interrupted whenever one of them had a question or an idea.

Alex worked on the finances. Good news. The wedding was way more profitable than they first thought. They made twenty-eight hundred that evening. Nearly every guest bought something to take with them, in addition to the wedding gifts. The average gift was just under fifty dollars. Their most profitable three hours ever.

Their to-do list grew:

> Hire a new employee
>
> Hire a bookkeeper
>
> Promote Ethan
>
> Check out health insurance plans for the bookstore
>
> Market bookstore weddings on the website

Market events that bring in large groups of customers

The book stock is low

Decide when to switch houses. The sooner, the better

Darlene will be close to the hospital

Tru might be moving in

The next morning Alex got an early start to the Portland area. She intended to fill the Forester with as many books as she could. She decided to go all the way out to Gresham, start there, and make her way back.

It took her nearly two hours to reach her first destination. She wasn't disappointed. The Gresham Goodwill book section looked like a merchandise dump. Maybe a bookstore had gone out of business. She packed four book boxes out of the first store. Time for a breakfast break.

She drove through McDonald's and parked. As she enjoyed her breakfast and coffee, her thoughts wandered. A light rain was falling, so she watched the raindrops on the windshield as she gave serious thought about their future as bookstore owners.

First, her business partner. What a shock to hear that she was pregnant. She admired Dar's decision, but the reality of it shook her up. The business would definitely suffer when babytime arrived. And possibly sooner. She might have to stop working early. Her health was way more important than the business. So they needed to get busy and do everything they could to ensure Dar, the baby, and the store remained in good health.

There was always so much to do that it took both of them working full-time to keep up. So they definitely needed a new employee, and more hours from Ethan, way more. It wasn't fair if it affected his school work. She better talk with him soon.

And of course, their financials were still shaky. But their recent success sort of proved that potentially they could make some serious money with the right business strategies. The goal was to get the buyers through the doors. People will buy books.

But before that plan became a reality, she and Dar needed to be prepared to contribute more money. New employees had to be paid. Meeting the payroll was always the problem.

Dar thought they should hire the staff way before the baby came so they would be ready whenever she left. That made total sense. It had to be the right employees, dedicated, trustworthy, and hard-working. That won't come cheap.

The rain started coming down harder. Shoot. She pulled her suv as close to the building as possible and ran in to use the restroom. Then she got a coffee refill and a couple cookies for the road. Onward.

She spotted a Salvation Army on her way south toward ultra-toney Lake Oswego. She parked close to the local Goodwill and ran through the increasingly heavy rain, shook herself off like a pooch, and started to browse around. A huge warehouse of a store. Lots of furniture.

That reminded her of their upcoming house switch. She was looking forward to moving into the loft. It was a great idea. She hadn't seen it since their big move-in. She wondered what kind of furniture Dar had purchased for it. They needed to get that switch done soon. Maybe Tru would help them. It wouldn't hurt to make him part of the family. Heavy lifting in addition to stud duties. Ha!

She took a quick look at the furniture for future reference and then found the books. A vast book room. She chose wisely and nearly filled the cart. Then she wandered through the Vintage shop. A bit overpriced, but she talked the manager into a bulk rate deal for a stack of 1960s novels still in excellent condition. She also bought a set of beautiful Desert Rose dishes for her new digs, circa 1960s. They packed them well for her.

The car was about two-thirds full now, still room for more books. Next stop was Tigard. About half a box. No rare books on the shelves. She found several other thrift shops. She had encountered many disgruntled customers complaining about the high prices for used clothes and shoes. Interesting. Books were priced the same as ever. A good buy at the current price. Disdain for books in general led to that policy. It worked for her. She found enough books to fill several more boxes.

If you figure 30 books per box, she had purchased nearly 300 books. She had spent about $450 of the store's money on books. Say they sold them for $10 each. That's about a $2,500 net profit, or about $8 per book. Not bad for this morning's unpaid work. And about $50 worth of gas, also out of her pocket.

Tomorrow she would place an Engram order for new books. They cost way more, but customers paid close to full price for them. And readers like new books. Three hundred books might cost her $2400, but they could make $15 per book, possibly making $4,500. That's why booksellers want bestselling authors on their shelves.

More guessing. Typically, a customer buys one new book and two used books. And often a magazine, a candy bar, and a greeting card. The net profit from that sale is about $35. Or some combination of merchandise that equals $35. So they needed about 15 of those customers per day. That didn't seem unreasonable.

She had lost track of how many books they had on hand. It's not too difficult to get a rough estimate by simply counting the number of shelves and, multiplying by 30, then adding the table counts.

The stock gets stale if it isn't moved around. So sale tables and seasonal reading choices are designed to feature books that aren't getting enough attention, or are lingering too long. The marketing theory relating to used books is that if they were sold once, they have intrinsic value. Remainders, and those darlings from the Dollar store are essentially losers. Nobody has read them. They are pretty placeholders. Don't fill the bookstore with books nobody wants to read.

If a bookstore is open 26 days per month and it makes $500 per day in profit, that's approximately $150,000 per year, which sounds respectable, until you realize that the skilled Silicon Valley tech worker could earn about $200,000, per year, which is why tech workers with good skills should stay away from buying bookstores. They aren't profitable. And it's also why employees shouldn't be drawn to bookstore jobs.

Minimum wage is $15 per hour, or $30,000 per

year, for a 40-hour work week. Most booksellers work part-time and are lucky to earn $15 per hour. So a store needs a lot of them. And as a rule, they come and go frequently.

Once the bookstore's finances are understood and you have a fair idea of what the store's contents are worth, it's easier to figure out how many customers need to walk through the door. And then it becomes clear why the bookstore needs merchandise for nonreaders. And it tells the owners how often they need to add more books. And it paints the grim picture of why bookselling is a labor of love.

She would stop off at the Dollar Store and try to buy more candy. There is such a good profit margin on quality candy. Hope that gig lasts.

On Thursday Darlene, with Tru in tow, rang Alex's doorbell at 8:30 am, armed with coffee and donuts. The big boyfriend reveal. Alex was impressed. He was maybe five-eleven, not quite six feet. Darlene was five-four. He was handsome in a cowboy construction worker way. Jeans, workbooks, short brown hair, alert eyes, seriously smitten with Darlene. What's not to like? An Oregon guy.

They quickly downed the coffee and gobbled up the donuts, even though Darlene looked a little peaked and fragile. Her red curls were a bit limp. They showed up for a look-see. Alex had cleaned up the cottage the previous night. They nosed through the plain rooms. Darlene exclaimed at the dining room built-ins and the mahogany sliders that opened the dining room and living room. Alex had never touched them. Tru examined them closely. He'd fix them up.

They admired the old kitchen and liked the bathroom. The main bedroom closet was okay for one person. They would add an armoire for Tru. The little bedroom was perfect for a child. The washer-dryer on the converted back porch was cold but useful. It was beginning to sound like couplehood for the two of them.

They went down to the basement and were totally in love. An extra bedroom and bath was a great family room space. TV and lounging couches, a place for kids to hang out. Yes, it was a family home. Dar and Tru were practically swooning over it and each other.

Excellent work, Starbucks. You've done it again. A sweet couple. Tru's do-over relationship. He would do it right this time. Alex was gritting her teeth. Watching lovers swoon was sort of sickening.

They trudged through the backyard and observed the play set. Tru decided he could make it safe. A one-car garage at the end of the driveway separated her house from the neighbor. Typical middle-aged house, especially if you ignore the mildew smell. They were sold. The paperwork would be completed by the same real estate agent who handled their previous deal.

It wasn't Alex's business to pry, so she would wait for Dar to tell her, but it did look like a permanent living situation was developing. A good start for a child on the way. Alex watched from the window as the couple left the house. They stopped at the sidewalk and glanced back at the large front porch. Tru enfolded Darlene into his arms as they looked at their future home.

That afternoon Darlene handed her keys to Alex, who hoofed it up to the loft for her look-see. The outside stairs opened into the great room. The large framed window looked out onto the street where she could see the Starbucks and the diner. Excellent.

The low window sills were wide, great for cat perches. They could spend a lot of time there. The room held the kitchen, a table, and plenty of room for a tv, a couch, a side chair, and bookshelves.

Darlene's art table and supply cabinet would go with her. Same with the computer desk eyesore. The rest of the furniture was okay. Alex wasn't sure she needed or wanted the tv couch. They'd take that too.

The bedroom was in the back. Furniture was

okay. The bath was good. The utility closet was fine too. It would be an easy move for Alex, just clothes and personal stuff would get moved. Darlene would need a small moving van. Tru would rent one, and with a friend, they could handle it. They decided they could make the switch in two weeks. Tru would help.

CHAPTER 4

Alex got some moving boxes from Home Depot and packed them up. She was surprised at how many boxes she filled, not counting clothes, which also went into boxes. She even had a couple boxes of books, for heaven's sake. She needed a small bookcase for them. Stacking them here and there wouldn't work now that most of her stuff would live in the big open room. She realized she would be more organized if she acquired a desk for all the papers and tech stuff she owned, in addition to her laptop, her iPad, her small printer, and her phone.

She also needed living room furniture. So she made a run to Portland and wandered through Crate & Barrel with a salesperson who helped her make sense out of living in one room. Luckily, she had photos and measurements with her. It would be a well-coordinated Crate & Barrel masterpiece of comfort and charm. The lady also convinced her that the existing dining table and chairs needed to go too, so Darlene was happy to take them with her.

The bossy salesperson even gave her paint chips

and the name of a painter who would come over and eliminate the boring white paint. So Alex agreed. Do it now so she could forget it for the next ten years or so. The lady even forced her charm into the bedroom. Alex left the store with a pile of bedding, side tables, appropriate sleepy-time artwork for the bedroom walls, and expensive pieces for the great room. Goodwill art is bad karma. The furniture would arrive in a few weeks.

Alex listened and learned. But when she saw the results, she was thrilled. Her new home had been transformed. It was more than just the room to walk through on her way to get something to eat or to go to bed. Her cats liked the loft better too, especially the huge windows overlooking the street. And the nearby trees.

Alex had shown the eager salesperson the 1960s dishes she had recently purchased. She approved of them. Quirky, but retro chic. The woman worked their colors into her palette, so the dishes now seemed to finally live in a perfect world. They even had their own hutch, so they were always actively part of the decor.

Alex admitted to Darlene that she was thrilled by her pretty new loft. She felt safe up there by herself, and although it was a large space, it had a cozy feel to it that really pleased her.

Darlene burbled about the cottage too. Tru

was painting and repairing some minor flaws, tricking out the family room, and working on their nursery. This was the construction slow time, meaning that he was collecting unemployment, and he had the skills to do what was needed. She convinced him that all the projects needed to be done soon. He agreed. Full speed ahead.

Darlene was also occupied with doctoring, getting tested, beginning prenatal classes, and working on yoga poses. So between the baby, overseeing the nursery, buying cute baby girl things, and working with Tru on what was turning into a monster of a renovation, she was neglecting her share of the bookstore work. She thought it was temporary, but as more awful problems were discovered, it was becoming clear that she was over-extended and overly tired. If she didn't slow down, her doctor would insist on complete bed rest.

Roof repairs turned into a new roof. Garage bracing turned into a garage gut job and workshop extension. The interior painting unveiled mold problems, so the drywall needed replacing. When the walls were opened up, active termites and rotten framework were discovered. Rotted eaves and leaky gutters needed to be replaced. The furnace croaked, the gas stove leaked, and the freezer stopped working. Even the Keurig smelled moldy, suggesting something was wrong in the kitchen too. The kitchen floor needed replacing. A leaky pipe was found dripping into the basement.

Most people speak of their house as having good bones. Unfortunately, this cottage had terrible bones.

So Dar moved into an extended-stay hotel and turned the house project over to Tru, who hired the contractor to finish the project.

Money was leaking through her fingers. So she had to tell Alex that she needed to get a real job for a few months to cover the expenses. Through her still active LinkedIn contacts, she got a three-month high-paying Silicon Valley contract. She worked remote from her quiet, well-appointed hotel nest while Tru helped the contractor and a handful of subs to get the cottage finished. Bottom line, she needed a leave of absence from book duties.

Alex tried to hide her disappointment and, admit it, her anger. Her business partner was derelict in her duties. Darlene knew full well that she was jeopardizing the store with herself-centered actions. How could she be so careless about walking away from the store?

Alex had to cope with it somehow. Darlene's abrupt absence left Alex and Ethan to run the bookstore alone. They had a long strategy session. She asked him if he had a trusted friend or relative who might be interested in working at the bookstore full-time.

Ethan's cousin Rishi Patel interviewed the next day. He appeared in good-looking preppy clothes, rimless glasses, was well-mannered, and had a dry sense of humor. He was 21, a graduate from Portland State with a philosophy degree. He had also disappointed his parents, who thought he was into computers. He was wiry, about 5-8, with dark hair and energy bursting at the seams. Definitely not the slouching, ill-clad, slow-moving stereotype of a philosophy major. Rishi could work Mondays through Fridays from 10 am until 7 pm. He'd have two meal breaks plus coffee, which he would receive gratis at either Starbucks or the cafe. His pay was $15 per hour. Hired! He could start immediately.

Ethan's pay was bumped to $16 per hour, and his job was now assistant manager. Ethan was in charge of his little sister, Ellen, called Ellie. He picked her up from school every day at 3:30. He had classes four mornings weekly.

So he asked if he could bring Ellie with him to the store after school. She was eager to work too. She could not go on the payroll until she was 15. However, if she was interested, she could learn how to clean up used books, do some shelving, and help with gift wrapping, all volunteer work. Aunty Alex would give her a regular allowance, and she, Ethan, and Rishi could run tabs at Starbucks and the diner for snacks and meals. Alex would pay their tabs out of her pocket without questions.

The three of them agreed. They would work as many hours as they could. Ethan said he and Ellie could work Tuesdays through Fridays from 4 until 7. He would work all day on Fridays and Saturdays. He would take off Sundays and Mondays.

Alex was so relieved. She now had reliable staff willing to work. She vowed to treat them well. And she let Ethan know how grateful she was for his quick thinking and his excellent recommendations.

Alex also added a contract bookkeeper/ accounting service specializing in small businesses. And she increased the days that the store would buy books from independent scouts.

Ethan then mentioned that his big sister, Serena, might be interested in working some bookstore hours. She was an event planner, but she could work at the desk and also oversee special events. She was single, a young professional with a winning smile. She would be an asset to the store. Alex hired her immediately as a bookseller,

$15 per hour, with meal privileges too.

Alex figured the meal tabs would appease the employees because they all should be earning more than minimum wage. And of course, they all had discounts of 30% on all book purchases. Meal tabs would be Alex's ongoing contribution to the bookstore. She would not be reimbursed.

Alex now had a staff, all Indian and all related to each other. She thought it was an excellent idea. They were loyal and trustworthy, knew each other, and worked well as a team. Now all they had to do was sell enough books to stay in business. Ethan trained the crew with minimal supervision from Alex.

Business continued to pick up as summer drew near. High tourist season began in late spring, although tourists always wandered around. Some tourists prefer the moody shores during the dreary winter.

According to the Seaside tourist board, millions of tourists visit Seaside every year, some just day-trippers, but many stay at least a night or two. This part of the Oregon coast was very popular. As a result, the standard of living was higher for the 6,500 hundred or so permanent residents than the lonelier beach towns in southern Oregon. Also, local politics tended to be more liberal. So environmentalists and nature lovers were welcome, and ex-Californians were not scolded quite as often.

However, that's not always true. One morning in April, a grumpy old pot-bellied man came into the bookstore with an angry look and a gun strapped to his back. He walked over to the large display of books celebrating Earth Day, nature books, animal books, books about trees, and most prominently, books related to climate change and environmentalism. He took one look and shouted, "Jesus H. Christ, would you look at this?" His wife was walking a couple paces behind him.

Alex picked up the phone and called the police. "No, it isn't exactly an emergency, yet. But there is a loud old guy with a gun in the store. He's angry. No, not brandishing it. Just making sure everybody sees it. Thank you."

Alex approached the man and said, "Welcome to Seaside Books. Is there something I can help you with?"

He glared at her and read her name tag. "Yeah, what's this lefty crap doing right here. It makes me sick! Oh, you're the owner. I heard a couple of California lesbians bought this place and turned it over to a bunch of Indians to run."

"I'm Alexia, the owner of this store. If you can't keep your voice down and your opinions to yourself, I'm asking you to leave my store."

"Oh yeah. It's a free country. Or at least it used to be. I can go into any store I want."

His wife came up to him and put her hand on his arm. "Now, Homer, you know what the doctor said."

He brushed her arm off, and turned on her. She backed off like he might hit her. Probably a regular occurrence, Alex thought.

"Get out, now. I mean it," she said, her anger matching his.

"You got no right…"

"Yes, I do. It looks like you're getting ready to hit this woman. That's reason enough."

At that point, a cop came through the door. Homer saw him immediately and swore again. "Son of a bitch."

The cop recognized him. "Homer, if you don't leave this store immediately, I will arrest you."

"What for?"

"Let's start with threatening a store owner. I just heard you making slurs about a minority group, calling her names, and displaying a gun in public. That's three serious charges. With your record, we're talking jail time."

"Oh, Jeez, I ain't done nothing yet."

"Let's keep it that way. This store is off-limits

as far as you are concerned. We patrol here. If I see you here again, I will arrest you. Got it? I'm serious."

He turned towards the door. His wife murmured, "I'm sorry." They left.

Alex was stunned. A guy with a gun just walked in and started swearing at her. In her bookstore, of all places. And his attitude. She had never been subjected to that language before.

Ethan came over. They sat on the stools and commiserated. Awful. He had heard it before. His family had been in the US for years. Unfortunately, their last name was Patel, like Smith or Nguyen. Gomez. Common. Slurs against successful women. That made them lesbians and commie sympathizers. Oregonians hated Californians because they had money, drove nice cars, and could go on vacation. Angry right-wingers. So ugly.

Life in a small town. Everybody knows your business.

In the meantime, Darleen was working at home, enjoying the quiet, and feeling a little guilty about it. She was making a ton of money on a quick turnaround project. But sitting at a laptop for hours wasn't great. So she timed herself, went to her baby classes, and stayed away from the bookstore. That worked. The estimated cottage job completion was six months away. Her due date was five. So Tru moved a portable crib and other necessities for a newborn's first months into the hotel apartment.

Her return to the bookstore looked doubtful. Alex might have to buy her out and become the sole owner. They would wait and see. Alex didn't tell her about the ugly incident with the angry man. Alex didn't tell her much these days. Dar was slipping out of the picture entirely.

Tru was balancing the renovation, his continuing unemployment, and his ex and kid visitation while making sure that the mother of his next child was okay. And a few other things that he wouldn't mention. He ended up with a bunch of responsibilities and no money. He moved out of the room he lived in and bunked with Darlene. That saved some money. The hotel room had a small kitchen so they could eat in. That saved Tru even more.

Tru was being pulled in so many directions. He still loved his first wife, Pauline, and the kids. There were four of them, two in school, a toddler and a one year old. He couldn't remember all their names. Pauline couldn't afford daycare so she didn't work. She received welfare and food stamps because Tru rarely paid child support. He wondered whether he should marry Darlene and suggest that his kids become part of their family.

The perfect solution for him because then the child support problem would end. Darlene had no idea yet. Nor did Pauline.

Tru's problems were common and predictable. He liked the ladies, and they liked him, maybe a little too much. He worked construction, but only half-heartedly, so he was first to be laid off. His money slid through his fingers. He meant well, he wanted to please everybody, but pleasing himself was most important.

Good news, finally, for the bookstore. A couple inquired about a wedding, and on its heels, another request. The first couple came in and met with Alex and Serena. They were young, not the ideal profile, as far as Alex was concerned. She explained that bookstore weddings were perfect for older couples not interested in receiving traditional wedding presents.

"Oh?" said the bride-to-be, "What difference does it make what kinda gifts the guests wanna bring? There's plenty a room to stack the gifts in the corner over there. And I'm thinking we could probly dance right down the aisles. You do have speakers, right?"

Alex tried to explain the concept of a bookstore wedding to the young woman and her embarrassed but silent young man. The bride had an alternate theory for every sentence. It was obvious that she was barely listening, and what she was hearing wasn't matching her needs. She became argumentative and surly.

"Ya don't push all these books outta the way? I mean, if you did, we could set up a buffet and have dancing. I just don't understand how you think people can hold a wedding here."

Finally, the groom said, "You see, we don't have much money for the wedding. When we saw we could have ours here for $500, we just jumped at the chance. We aren't interested in books, but we'd love to get married here."

"I'm sorry," said Alex, "I don't think this is the right venue for your wedding. There is no room for dancing, no room for meal service, no speakers in the bookstore, and no DJ. And the appeal of the bookstore wedding is for the guests to buy books for the couple. They choose books for the bride and groom on the wedding day. Convenient and something the bride and groom would appreciate."

"Ugh, I don't want no books cluttering up my house," said the now angry young woman, making a face. "That just sounds like a trick to me. A scam to get people to buy books."

Alex continued, ignoring the rudeness, "As I said, this isn't the right venue for you. But thank you for coming in. If you ever need something to read, we're here."

"You know what? I don't think I like this place at all." They left in a hurry.

Dead silence until the bridezilla-in-training left the building. And then both Alex and Serena started chuckling. "You know," said Serena, "that's the perfect example of every event planner's worst nightmare. She will be writing up her Yelp review before she even gets home."

The next couple was older, and they loved the idea of a bookstore wedding for all the right reasons. Alex thought it sounded like a repeat of their first experience. The couple toured the store and the area where the ceremony would take place. They wanted to be married the first weekend in June, if possible. Alex was delighted to have Serena take over the planning with them.

Other requests came along. Summer weddings are popular along the coast. Alex hadn't been aware of it. Several events were booked. They ensured the store looked its best, with many signs so guests could easily find what they sought. Alex went scouting to find books that might make good wedding gifts.

Again, all staff, including Ellie, were on hand for the next wedding wearing shades of blue. Serena was the hostess. Her name was an excellent description of her style. This group of guests were somewhat at sea because, after so many years of traditional weddings, it was difficult to throw the shackles off.

They were a mature group of maybe 30 guests. The reception table was set against the back wall. In addition to a delicious tray of cupcakes, their caterer also placed tiny tea sandwiches, warmed canapés, and small delicacies on toothpicks. It all fit onto small plates. Champagne glasses of plastic appeared. The bottles on ice. And appropriate flowers.

The chairs were placed for comfort. The music again was an iPhone playlist, this time provided by Serena. During the previous meeting, when asked about music, the happy couple grinned, looked around, and said, "How silly of us to expect an organist."

The couple permitted Rishi to take some photos. Serena showed them a small Shutterfly photo book. For $200, Rishi would create one for the couple. They were delighted.

An elderly judge, a family member, did the honors so the wedding vows were quick, charming and fun. He laced the necessary words with wisdom and short reminiscences. He was a hit.

Since 30 guests couldn't all crowd around the table at once, a line formed. Once seated with their plates of finger food, Serena came around with the champagne on a tray. Many guests preferred to stand. So the reception looked like a successful cocktail party, with guests walking and talking to each other and the couple doing the same. There was much laughter and happiness, no sitting at tables with strangers waiting for the next thing, like a traditional wedding with its long interludes.

When each guest had polished off a sufficient amount of champagne, Serena explained that it was time to explore the bookstore to choose some books for the happy couple. Lots of book talk ensued as the guests began to wander around. This was serious business. And after such a lovely wedding party, they were in a generous mood.

Ellie and Rishi were busy wrapping up the gifts. Ethan helped guests find books, and Alex was the cashier. Serena wandered, answering questions about future parties. Could they hold a birthday party here? The mahjong players were celebrating something. One guest thought a retirement party might be perfect here. Serena handed out her business cards and made notes to follow up with phone calls next week.

By ten pm the last guest had left the store. The wedding had been an enormous success. Better than they had even hoped for. And the potential for future parties was stunning. Alex was in such a good mood. Hugging and thanking the staff, she declared bonuses for all.

A late night, on top of a full day. Nice to be able to get home so easily. The cats greeted her and told her it was past time for their evening snack.

She changed into her jammies and robe and poured herself a glass of wine. Time for her snack and to put her feet up. Retail work is so very different. Even the exhaustion felt different. Smiling, making polite conversation with total strangers. Ugh. She was so tired she didn't even have time to read.

CHAPTER 5

The baby came in July, early but reluctantly. Darlene wasn't quite ready. It took her by surprise. Her contract gig had been extended, so she was working away at her laptop. Just like she had in the Bay Area. Once again she was caught up in the snare that they had worked so hard to run away from. And then the baby came. She was handing off her job between contractions. She promised to be back as soon as she could.

Her calls to Tru went unanswered. So she left texts and voicemails. He had promised to be on hand for the big day, but so far, he was a missing person. Obviously, the big day caught him by surprise too.

Darlene was on good terms with the hotel staff by this point. They knew her well and liked her. So when she called the front desk needing a ride, a car and driver were provided. One of the staff would stay with her until Tru could be located.

After her shift was over, the hotel staff member recalled that Darlene was part owner of Seaside Books. She called them and Alex came right over. Rishi and Serena were on hand so she left the store in good shape.

By the time Alex showed up, Darlene had been in labor for hours and was exhausted. The doctors were conferring. So Alex stayed with her, held her hand, and tried to be brave for her. What a frustrating experience. Between contractions, Darlene swore never to get pregnant again. They both swore at Tru for the continuing radio silence.

The doctors decided that the best course of action was a C-section. Alex was in the waiting room when Tru showed up. Apologetic. He had turned off his phone so he didn't hear the call come in. A family emergency.

Yeah right, thought Alex. People always turn their phones off when they have a family emergency. Alex just said, "Gimme a break." And rolled her eyes.

He said, "I'm here now. You can leave if you want to."

"I'm staying."

They sat in silence for a while. Then Tru went into the hall and made phone calls. Lots of them, angry, hurtful calls. Alex tried not to listen. Tru apparently had a complicated personal life. She didn't want to know about it.

The doctor showed up looking for Alex. Tru

butted in. He was the boyfriend and the father. The doctor spoke to them both at the same time. The mom and baby girl were both okay. Just exhausted. They would stay in the hospital for a couple of nights at least. The baby would be in the nursery soon. The viewing station was down the hall. Darlene was in recovery, asleep. They could see her when she woke up.

Tru paced. Alex ignored him.

Finally, he said, "Are you staying?"

"Yes."

"Well, tell her I'm sorry I wasn't here. I'll be back soon. Just got a few things to check on."

"Tell her yourself."

"Bitch."

"Jerk."

He left.

Alex was so irritated at Tru. Like so many guys, his screwed-up life was always most important. She wasn't making any apologies for that jerk. He'd been mooching off of Darlene ever since she met him.

She checked in with Ethan. She might be a while. She wanted to make sure Darlene was okay. Not sure how long it would take.

A few hours later, Dar was in her room, still

sleepy but okay. The nurses would be in soon with the baby. Alex told her she'd be back the next morning but call if she needed anything.

Darlene and the baby left the hospital after a few days of recovery. Tru picked her up, got her back to the hotel, and had to leave. She called Alex. They decided she would come by in the mornings after Tru cleared out. She'd help her with the baby every morning until she felt well enough to be on her own. Alex didn't have to be at the bookstore until noon.

So that became the routine. Alex would come by around 9, do chores, run a load of laundry, and pick up stuff at the pharmacy or grocery store. Bathe the baby, who was very cute already. Then she'd make Dar a sandwich and take off for the store.

Things weren't great between Darlene and Tru. Obviously. She wasn't sure whether Tru would be in her life much longer. He wasn't interested in the baby or her. He ignored the fact that she needed help, and Alex was coming over and spending three hours with her before doing eight hours at the store.

"So what's your point, Dar? I'm busy too. This kid is your idea, remember?"

He had suggested they get married. When she said he had to get his personal life in order first, he exploded. To him, marrying Dar was the answer to getting his personal life in order. Once the house was done, he could take his kids back. They could bunk downstairs, so no more child support. Then his ex might stop bugging him.

Darlene was appalled. His kids living with her, while he came and went? That wasn't going to happen. She wasn't about to solve all Tru's problems with her house and her money. And end up living a nightmare life with stepkids and a husband who probably would cheat on her. With his ex. Nope. Not interested.

Once she was well again, she'd be fine. If she had to hire a housekeeper for a while, she would. But marriage was off the table.

Darlene realized that she had a lot of decisions to make. She was torn between the bookstore life and the tech world. In the short time she was back in tech again, she had earned a great deal of money. That made her feel better about the cottage. It would be a good house for her and her baby, but it would be better with a partner. Tru was the wrong one.

She would never make enough money at the bookstore to properly raise her little girl, so she'd have to rely on her nest egg. That was a very uncomfortable thought. Could she do both for a while? And raise a baby?

The cottage was finally completed. The furniture and Darlene's personal things were unpacked by her and the housekeeper's husband. Dar loved the place. The basement had been completed as an apartment. It had an outside entrance and a small kitchen, one large bedroom and a tv sitting room.

Darlene didn't remember saying yes to it becoming an apartment. But now that gave her an idea. She'd offer it to her housekeeper and her husband. Make her a deal that included the apartment. The housekeeper said yes and Darlene was relieved. That was a much better use of it than what Tru had in mind.

She and Tru got into a huge fight. He wanted to move in with her. They could work things out. She didn't think they could. Tru bellowed that she owed him all the hours he worked on the house. She countered that he owed her child support. He reminded her that he was a sperm donor, not the father. It went on like that until Darlene was fed up with him. She knew he was broke and in debt, and his family life was a mess. But it wasn't her problem to solve. And he hadn't shown any interest in the baby. They had no future together. She told him it was over.

She talked to the contractor about Tru's contribution to the job. He looked at her over the rim of his glasses. He paid Tru hourly as a sub out of the contract money. She, in reality, had already paid him. The contractor thought she knew that. And frankly, Tru hadn't been around all that much. Not too reliable.

She decided to concentrate on the baby for a while instead of jumping back into full-time employment or going back to the bookstore. Let the housekeeper take care of them both. Time to focus on the little one.

When Alex found out that Dar had not set a date to come back to the bookstore, she was shocked. What? How could that be? Was Dar abandoning their business relationship? Could she walk away and pick it up again at a more convenient time? Business partners weren't supposed to do that. There were essential jobs that she could do from home at her convenience. She could contribute that way for a while. It would help. Dar shook her head.

As far as Alex was concerned, Dar had to commit. Was she in or out? She needed to make that decision. They both knew how difficult it was for her to make big decisions. If she wanted out, Alex would have to buy her share of the business. She hadn't been contributing anything to the business for over six months. They didn't want to go to an attorney for help, but somehow they needed to work out this complication.

Dar argued that Alex was pushing her too

quickly. The bookstore dream was originally hers, after all. She was the one who convinced Alex to do it. Now, she needed more time to decide whether to give it up.

They settled on three months. If Dar still hadn't come to a decision by then, they would hire someone to figure out how much Alex would have to pay her for her share. Meanwhile, Alex was working like mad, trying to keep the business afloat.

Alex had no idea that it would come to this. She knew that small businesses had a hard time at first. But how often did one partner just walk away from a business and then expect to get her share back? Alex couldn't answer that. The only thing she could do was to keep going and hope things would work out.

No matter what happened, it looked like this might be the end of their friendship as well. Alex figured she couldn't dwell on that. No time to fret about her personal life. She had sunk a lot of money into the business. Luckily, Dar paid her for the cottage before either of them knew how much she was going to spend renovating it. That was another complication.

As she sat in her cozy loft watching the rain come down on the street below, she often thought of the Bay Area. But those thoughts turned sour when she remembered the pandemic. The isolation, hours on end working at her laptop, a grocery run, and a car coffee might be the highlight of the week.

The bookstore work was different. She never knew what was coming up next. Or who she might meet up with. She wasn't sitting at her laptop day after day either. The pawnbroker, for example, reminding her of a tv show. And that big oldvguy with the ugly mouth, the bad attitude and a gun. Sheesh. She still had scary moments thinking about that incident. But she had to admit that life was more exciting day by day now. Don't let the rain, the dark clouds, the fog, and her never-ending loneliness get to her.

One morning Alex decided to spend a few minutes at the beach with her morning coffee. Broadway and the prom were often crowded with visitors. Seaside's best days were in late summer and early fall. Sunny, mild temperatures and soft breezes.

She stopped at the commemorative statue of Lewis and Clark, which was located at the other end of Broadway. A bronze statue of two young men in rough clothes standing together looking at the Pacific Ocean. Clark had a long gun planted by his foot. Lewis carried his journal open in his hands. The statue is called 'The End of the Trail.'

The Corps of Discovery Expedition began in Missouri in 1803. It took Lewis and Clark and a group of explorers two years to reach what is now called Seaside, Oregon. The enduring memories of that epic journey were recorded in Lewis's journal. It wasn't just his words. There are sketches, maps, lists, renderings of animals, faces, the various boats they used, a record of all the simple artifacts of their daily lives along the way. That's what made the trip so memorable. The stored knowledge in Lewis's journal. The importance of books cannot be overstated.

Seaside was now filled with hotels, motels, apartments, shops, eateries, and bars, all things that appeal to the ever-present tourists who roamed the streets, the prom and the long shoreline. Alex guessed that most of them didn't even notice the significant statue in their midst. She did hope, however, that they wandered down Broadway to her bookstore.

Alex had been living in Seaside for a year now. The end of the trail. She thought back to those very first days. It was early summer, but it wasn't all that warm, as she recalled. It was her first realization that the weather would be a lot different in the Pacific Northwest.

She and Darlene had driven up together, each in her own car filled with personal stuff. They made it a two-day trip, stopping the first night in Ashland, Oregon, an odd town devoted to theater. Tourists come from all over to attend open-air Shakespeare plays, eat great food, and essentially live in a theatrical fantasy world. They vowed to go back and spend more time there.

The next morning they drove Highway 1 along the coast enjoying the Oregon shore. They drove past gorgeous scenery, rough seas, and small, fogbound towns, one after the other, until, finally, they entered Seaside, their choice to settle and open a bookstore.

Alex had never been to Oregon, so this introduction was quite impressive. By the time they reached Seaside, Alex was aware of how different the freezing cold shoreline was. The tide swings were so evident. When the tide went out, the swells were very far away. The waves and clouds seemed to blend. So much gray. It was remarkable.

Seaside was built up with apartments and hotels. So it was deceptive. It was a small town with a huge and very temporary population.

Alex and Darlene had purchased several books on starting a bookstore. Good thing. The information seemed straightforward. There were guidelines, forms, advice, and examples of store layouts. All interesting. They talked about the information they had gleaned from it. Neither of them had ever worked in a bookstore.

In thinking back over those days, Alex felt good. They did it. They turned a dream into reality, an amazing feat since they did it using instruction manuals and luck. And, of course, pockets full of cash. They had both sold their homes in San Jose. They had bank accounts, stock portfolios, IRAs, checkbooks, and credit cards. All handy when starting a business. Things were supposed to be cheaper in Seaside. They were counting on that. Nevertheless, it had been a very expensive dream.

They left behind friends, workmates, relatives, memories, ex-boyfriends, and the familiar things that pleased or annoyed them. That's the price you pay to walk away, relocate, and start a new life. Often she wondered what it really was that convinced them to do it. Life had been comfortable, secure, and predictable. But they were living somebody else's dream in the Bay Area. They wanted to go to Seaside and open a bookstore. Their dream.

CHAPTER 6

Alex was eagerly awaiting the monthly financial report from the accountant. She anticipated hearing that they had a very good month. They had several special events, including two kid birthday parties, an excellent retirement party, and a wedding. Books left the store by the bagful, many of them way over the $35 average.

It was becoming a constant battle to keep enough stock on hand. Children's books were difficult to find used because they got beat up so badly by the first owner. FAlex didn't want to sell used books with teeth marks, especially children's books. They always made sure books were spotless before going out on the shelves. As a result, they ordered most of the kid books new. And the store now bought books from book scouts every day. The scouts learned quickly what they could sell to Seaside Books.

So there was usually a good stack of used books for Ellie to work on. Ethan showed her how to find out the retail sale price for each book. She caught on quickly. And she always alerted Ethan when a book seemed more valuable than usual.

Ellie also went through catalogs, both print and online, and suggested book titles for the young adult section. She was 13 now, so her expertise in that area was appreciated. She kept track of her hours on book business, and her allowance was adjusted accordingly.

Ethan never mentioned his parents or other relatives. Apparently, they had become accustomed to the fact that they had raised a group of booksellers. They were pleased that Ellie was at the store rather than running around with her girlfriends. Ellie, so far, was not complaining.

The financials were good news. Alex's goal for the store was $500 per day or 13k for the month. They had scrambled and made just over that for two months in a row now. It was the special events that made the difference. Without them they staggered along at about $300 per day. The salary figure was over 90k per year, the most significant expense. The store needed 150k per year to make payroll and stay in business.

Alex wanted to hire a part-time worker for the holidays. It was risky to the bottom line, but she didn't want to overwork her crew. If Darlene could come back, even for a few hours per day, it would make a difference. Maybe she could start by making cards and bookmarks at home. Even that would help. She would check in with

Darlene.

Then Alex started thinking about herself. She looked haggard. Mainly because she was tired most of the time. Her hair needed cutting. Gray strands were poking up. Her wardrobe was the worst. Her employees all out-dressed her. Even Ellie looked more professional than she did.

Maybe she needed a week off and some renovation. It's not unheard of to take a little time off occasionally, but she didn't think it was fair for the crew to work short-handed for a week.

Staff meetings were Tuesday nights at seven. They were seated around the table on the stage with pizza. Everybody checked in, including Ellie. All problems on the table. Ideas to improve were agreed on, and new suggestions kicked around. So Alex brought up her idea of taking a week off to get spruced up a little. They listened in silence. When she finished, they looked at each other, then stood up and started clapping, then marching round the table cheering.

When the group finally settled down, Alex said, "I take it, that's a yes."

They even decided that she should leave immediately to go to Portland, stay at a nice hotel, do a spa day, and definitely have an excellent relaxing time. Ellie would look in on the cats, feed them, litter box, playtime, the whole deal. Ethan, Rishi and Serena could handle the store.

So Alex booked a room at the Benson in downtown Portland. And a spa day nearby, with time at their hair salon. Good start. The spa took all day. She fell into bed after a delicious in-room dinner. And slept soundly.

The next morning at breakfast she looked closely at the downtown map. Good shopping close by. Might as well get some new clothes to match the new hairstyle. The stylist had cut off her long hair, which took ten years off. She suggested a short, blunt cut and blond highlights to minimize the gray. Easy to take care of and flattering. Okay.

She wandered over to the Galleria shops and found one that looked promising. The clerk helped her find some business casual outfits, as she called them. Slacks, tops with jackets, and no button sweaters. Good fitting jeans for very casual days, yoga pants, not too tight, with long sweaters. Age appropriate. Alex liked all of it. She would now have a wardrobe that belonged in a bookstore.

The next day she took care of the shoe problem quickly. Now it was time for some leisure. Since she was alone, dinners out were not a thing. She didn't like eating alone at night in some fancy restaurant, even if it was the Benson. So breakfast, lunches, and coffees. She spotted a combo bookstore, Starbucks, called Murphy's Books near the Galleria.

She went in, liked it. Much smaller than her store. Good idea to be connected to Starbucks. She wandered around, bought a copy of the Oregonian and a coffee, and took a seat. Settled in to read the headlines.

A few minutes later a middle-aged woman, like herself, came over and said, "Good morning, could I ask you a question?"

Alex smiled back, "Sure."

The woman said, "Hi, I'm Murf. I own this store. You look familiar to me. Are you the owner of that new bookstore in Seaside?"

Totally surprised, Alex answered, "Why, yes, yes I am. How did you know that? Please, sit down."

Murf took a seat. "Actually, I've been in your store a couple times. I make runs over that way quite often. I heard that you and your partner are doing well. Book news travels, you know."

Alex laughed. "I had no idea."

"Oh yes, you are a celebrity. Remember those books you sold at the pawnshop?"

"Oh, sure. Now that you mention it, I do."

"Well," Murf continued, "he's a friend of mine. He told me about you two walking in with the books. He was so surprised. Tell me, are you a rare book dealer?"

"No, just a bookseller, new to the business. Did we get taken on that sale?"

"Not at all, you caught him by surprise. If he had had more time, you might have gotten less. You did well, I think."

"That's good. We had no idea what they might be worth. We picked them up at the Goodwill of all places. It was a mistake on their part. I hear Goodwill is trying to do a better job of identifying valuable things. They blew it."

Murf continued, "I deal in rare books. So, yes, it's unusual when they pop up at a thrift shop. But still a good story. And then we hear that you are holding weddings in your store. That's simply brilliant."

"Yes, we are, it's working well. I can't take credit for the idea. A customer asked us about getting married in our store. She had it all figured out. We've done a couple kid parties and a retirement party too. The guests have to like books. It's a money maker for us."

Murf was thinking, "It's a tough business these days. I'm happy to know you are doing well. If you ever find books you have questions about,

I can help you. Here's my card." She pushed it across the table.

"Thanks, I appreciate that. Say hello the next time you're in town." She gave Murf her card.

It was time for Alex to get back to the hotel. She was pleased with that meetup. She had just learned something important. But not sure just what it was.

She also paid a visit to Powell's, just up the street a few blocks from the Benson. What a huge, sprawling store. Impossible to see in one visit. So busy, books stacked everywhere. And beautiful bookcases filled with books. Lots of books, but tidy. No musty shelves. Impressive. And as they say: Legendary bookstore. Definitely worth seeing.

She walked through the Pearl District. Saw lots of interesting shops, bars, restaurants, breweries. Plenty for a couple to do. Somewhat wistfully, she returned to her hotel, ordered room service, and called it a night. It had been a relaxing couple of days. Now she was eager to get back home and tackle something. Not quite sure what, but something. She just kept getting that feeling. Something was going to change.

Alex showed up at the store Friday afternoon.

Everybody was on hand and happy to see her. They loved her new clothes and her hair style. She looked like a younger store owner. And, yes, they missed her. She told them that she had decided to hire a part-timer for the holidays. She would simply put a 'help wanted' sign in the window and see who inquired. Rather old-fashioned, but this is an old-fashioned business. Okay with them.

The following Tuesday morning, Alex put the sign up, and promptly forgot it. Fall was underway, the skies were gray, the clouds low and the rain nearly a permanent fixture. She was wandering around the store looking at the ceiling, which was high. She was thinking of where she could install a spiral staircase to the loft. It was tiresome to get wet every morning going from the loft to the bookstore.

She was on the stage trying to decide which part of the loft was over it when she heard the door open. It was a regular customer, a middle-aged man, quiet, with a slow smile. He was about 5-10, usually wore a suit and an overcoat, and carried an umbrella.

She waved to him, wishing she remembered his name. Was it an English-sounding name, like maybe Charles? She giggled. What if his last name was King? He usually wandered through the mystery section so she could continue her investigation of the ceiling a while longer.

Then she thought, what about a regular staircase? Wouldn't that be lovely? There was plenty of room upstairs for a staircase but not as much space in the store. It would probably cost a fortune too. Was it worth it?

As she was moseying back to the desk, the customer interrupted her. He had a couple books and was ready to pay for them. But small talk first.

He said, "I didn't see you last week when I was here. Glad to see you are back and looking so well."

"Why, thank you. I took a week off. I had a nice break in Portland." She looked down. She was holding his credit card. Oh, that's right, it was Benjamin Derby, pronounced Darby. Yes, now she remembered the gang talking about him. He was English, maybe. And he was purchasing a lovely used hardback of a Le Carre novel, The Constant Gardener: a brilliant British mystery, a classic.

He smiled, "Ah, off on holiday then. Good for you."

She plopped the book into a store handle bag and handed it to him with his receipt and credit card. She said, "Here you go. It's always nice to see you, Mr. Derby."

He hesitated for a moment and then looked her in the eye. "I do have another question. I noticed the sign in the window. You need a bookseller? Might I apply for the job?"

That took Alex by complete surprise. "Oh? Would you be interested in actually working here? As a bookseller? Do you have any experience with books? Or retail? It's not that difficult, of course. But…"

"No, I've never worked in retail. But I have lots of work experience. And I do love books."

She reached under the counter, pulled out an application form, and said, "Of course, I'd be happy to talk to you about the job. Here's an application. You can fill it out here or take it with you and bring it back later. You are the first to apply."

He said, "I'll just pop over to Starbucks and fill it out. Do you mind if I bring it back in an hour or so?"

"Sure, we could talk then. Rishi will be here."

"Thanks." He grinned. "You know, I've been retired for a while. This is kind of exciting, applying for a job. I'll see you in a bit then."

Alex watched him leave the store. Benjamin Derby working here, she thought. Why the hell not? He seemed like the bookstore type. The others talked about him. They liked him. An older man in the store. British, sort of, just the faintest accent. Book lover. Interesting. She wondered what he had done for a living. She'd soon find out.

When Rishi showed up, Alex told him Mr. Derby was applying for the bookseller job. What did he think about that?

Rishi gave it a minute. "Ya know, it might be a good choice. He's definitely reliable. And something tells me he doesn't need the money. A good thing. He's quiet, not a know-it-all. We get quite a few of them. I approve. A much better choice than a local teenager, I think."

"If you are okay here, I'll wander over to Starbucks and talk to him there. He's filling out the application."

"Sure, go ahead."

So Alex ran over. She found Mr. Derby and told him she'd get a coffee and join him. They could talk here. He was surprised and pleased. He took a few minutes before she returned to look over his application and take a few breaths.

Starbucks knew her by sight, knew her order, and asked if she wanted a pastry. She said no. They put her drink on the tab, and she was back quickly.

She sat down across from him and smiled. He did too, and appeared to be just a bit nervous. Job interviews are tense. That's the way it goes.

She began by explaining the job, the training, and the hours. She figured between twenty and thirty per week. It would depend on how busy they would be. She'd like him to come in Thursday through Sunday. Five-hour shifts. If they booked any parties, she'd like him to work those too. The pay would be $12 per hour, a 30% book discount, and coffee breaks, and one meal at the diner paid.

He understood. Then they looked at his application. He was a widower from Toledo. He had owned his small accounting firm for years and dissolved it when his wife died and he moved to Seaside. Been here a year or so. Needed something to do.

She said, "I'm sorry for your loss. Living alone can be difficult."

"Yes, it is. Thank you."

She continued, "So you think working in a bookstore might be interesting?"

"Yes, I suppose I could go back to work as an accountant and make more money, but it's deadly dull, you know."

She nodded. "Standing for long hours is difficult

too. And we do move books around. There's some lifting, some dirty work. And the customers. They can be trying. We must be nice to them always. I don't think you'd have a problem there. What about standing? Would that be a problem?"

"Oh no. None of it would bother me at all. I'd look forward to it."

She noted his education. Grew up in Massachusetts, with an accounting degree from Boston College.

She said, "Tell me about books. How you feel about them."

He loved books. They were his companions now. When he was young, he wanted to be an English teacher so he could talk about books, but his folks convinced him that making money was more important than talking about books. Now that he had a little money and was retired, maybe it was time to indulge himself.

They talked a bit more. It became clear that he didn't know a thing about the business end but that didn't matter. He would be good with the customers. He was soft-spoken and polite. Well-educated. A very good fit with the staff. She hired him. He would start Thursday at two.

CHAPTER 7

Benjamin Derby showed up for work on Thursday fifteen minutes early. Rishi met him at the desk. He held out his hand, and they shook. Rishi said, "Welcome, Mr. Derby. Glad to have you with us."

"Please call me Ben," he said. "I'm happy to be here."

He filled out the forms. Then the training began. Rishi was very thorough. He started by showing Ben a book, looking it over the way a bookseller might. They looked at several, and then Ben showed him one, pointing out the condition, the dust jacket, and the printing information. Then they went through the store carefully. Rishi was talking, and Ben was observing. There's so much thought that goes into putting books on shelves. Ben nodded and asked appropriate questions.

Next, Rishi handed Ben off to Ellie, who had just come in. She would teach him how to get the used books ready for shelving. He'd work with her until dinner break.

Alex showed up, and they all chatted for a while.

When a group of customers came in, Rishi and Alex broke off to head to the front of the store. It had been a slow day. Maybe things would pick up now. Serena was coming in at 5:30 to see a couple about a wedding.

It would take a week before Ben would be fully trained. And then he'd work with another employee at the cash register for a while. It takes time to become a confident and experienced employee, something that most customers don't see. Customers expect a certain amount of insight from employees. It comes with experience. Ben would be good at it, just like the others. Alex was very proud of her staff. When she started the business, she had no idea how important the team was to the store's success. Now she did.

It was time for Alex to learn a new skill. She decided to look into buying and selling rare books. She had no idea where the line was between typical and rare books. She knew they were miles apart. So there was probably a middle area of books, older books that held or increased their value but didn't qualify for 'rare' status. That was going to be her starting point. The first thing she did was to ask Ethan about the used books that came into the store that appeared to be worth more than their original selling price.

Ethan perked up. "Oh, I've been meaning to ask

you that very question. I have a stack of them. We don't get them too often. Let's see," he was looking around behind the counter. "Hmm, they are in a box somewhere," he checked various places for them. Finally he asked Ellie about them.

She came over and peeked into the gift wrap closet. On the bottom of it stood a box, nearly filled with books. "Here you go. I was wondering when somebody was going to look at them."

Alex was pleased. "Thanks, Ellie, for taking such good care of them. Ethan, when you get a chance, would you take them up to the loft? I want to take a look at them. Price them myself.

"I think we need a category for collectible and signed books. Do you know, offhand, if we have any books scattered around the shelves that might qualify for special shelving?"

"Yes, I do, as a matter of fact. I'll hunt them up."

"Good. I think 'collectible books' might be of special interest for the holidays."

She had been studying online about collecting and selling rare books. This was going to be the store's next area of expertise. She still remembered that huge profit they got from the pawnbroker. Just where were those books out there in the world, and how could she get her hands on a few more of them?

Serena booked another wedding. Again, a middle-aged couple who wanted a small party for a few friends and family. Books as gifts would satisfy the urge that friends had to get them something. An easy, fun and inexpensive wedding. Serena had also booked several office parties. Instead of the tired old white elephant parties, they could draw names and buy a book for a colleague. And a bonus, not too much boozing.

She had also created a package deal where the store catered a very light buffet for 25 guests for an extra $400. Several choices fit the season or the event. The hosts just showed up. The store was becoming quite adept at throwing simple parties for any occasion. But the parties meant more pressure to keep the inventory growing.

Alex was also becoming more experienced at finding large lots of good used books. She was thinking of asking Ben if he'd be interested in scouting with her one or two mornings a week when the store was quiet. She could use someone to help with the heavy lifting, navigating, and negotiating. He had the look of experience she needed. He said yes, he'd be delighted.

She had made some connections and now got leads on individuals who needed to get rid of book collections. Lots of reasons for that. Estate sales. Kids cleaning out the parents' house or their own house. Folks just running out of room and eventually needing help selling off all or part of their libraries. She scheduled one for Monday morning, having no real idea what she was doing, winging it.

Alex and Ben headed down the highway past Cannon Beach and found the house in an older tract of nice places facing the shore. A young man answered the door. Alex introduced herself and Ben. He looked relieved to see two friendly-looking people at the door. He invited them in.

He was clearing out his folks' house to put on the market and wanted to sell off their book collection. She explained that they needed to look at them first to decide whether they could use them.

He led them into the living room. One wall was lined with books. The dining room also had bookshelves filled with books.

"I'm hoping to make a deal for the whole lot," he said.

Alex answered, "We'll take a look and let you know. Give us a few minutes."

"Okay, I'll be in the kitchen if you need anything."

The living room was tidy. It had an unused feel to it. Sort of old-fashioned traditional furniture. Nice old oriental rug, knickknacks, dusty throw pillows. And the books. Alex took one look.

"Oh, oh," she said. Ben glanced at her and then at the books. Tidy rows of a Readers Digest collection. The deluxe edition, with the leather look. Gold printing. Several shelves worth. Then came the Book of the Month. Same thing. Alex pulled one off the shelf to show Ben. Inside the cover at the bottom. Book club. Feel them, lighter weight, the boards made from flimsy cardboard. They wouldn't be interested in any of them.

They moved to the dining room. Slightly more interesting. They found lots of mass-market paperbacks, dog-eared, many with bent spines, a huge collection of National Geographics, and a pile of Life magazines. She looked at the Nancy Drew mysteries. They weren't in good shape. Neither were the Hardy boys. So far, nothing of interest.

Then she spotted a shelf full of Agatha Christie mysteries, early ones. She pointed to those. They were all paperbacks. She would take those. And finally, a collection of children's books. She looked closely at them. There were maybe 30 or more picture books. No torn pages, crayon, or teeth marks. Nice old books. A very old dictionary, yes. Some hardbound atlases, yes. A family Bible, no. And a shelf full of old novels, several in slipcases. Yes to all of those. She would pay about $150 for the lot. Ben just nodded. He was still in learning mode.

Alex called out to the young man and told him what they'd like to buy.

"That's all?" he asked. "Not the nice books in the living room? I thought they might be worth a lot."

"Sorry, not to me. They are book club editions. We don't sell them in our store."

"Oh, bummer. Do any stores? I was hoping the books would all be gone today."

Alex felt sorry for him. She told him to call around. Describe the books. Do the same with the thrift stores. They might take them. But ask before you haul them down there. Maybe advertise them. Somebody might be interested.

He was becoming surly. He figured she must not know what she was talking about. His folks always said how valuable the books were. Their pride and joy. His legacy.

She asked if he was interested in selling the books she wanted.

He said, "Whatever."

Ben said he'd get the cartons. They'd pack them up. He left and was back almost immediately. The kid was still whining about the books. Alex was listening patiently.

"Perhaps a family member would be interested in them for sentimental reasons."

"That would be me. I'm the only family member," he sneered. "I don't want none of that shit. And I think you are probably lying."

"You might want to take a quick look at each book. Sometimes folks stash cash in them. And especially bibles. There's a family Bible on the bottom shelf. You might want to look at that one too."

"Oh, yeah?" he said. "Well, you didn't know my folks. Penny pinchers. They wouldn't do that."

"Your choice." Ben was quickly packing the books. There would be maybe four or five boxes. They both watched him. He handed the Bible to the kid, who just held it. It was heavy. Alex thought, good idea. It would keep him from throwing something.

The kid didn't help Ben to carry any boxes to the car. Alex held the door. When he was finished, Alex counted out $150 in cash and handed it to him. He looked at her, still holding the Bible. She placed the money on the big book, said thank you, and left.

She heard the door slam behind her.

Ben was behind the wheel, the engine running. He backed out quickly onto the street and took off. As soon as they were out of sight, he sighed.

"Well, boss, that was interesting. I didn't know I was riding shotgun with no weapon."

"Right? I'm sure glad there were two of us. He was sincerely pissed. Thanks for keeping such a cool head. That was getting kinda dicey."

Ben said, "Sure was. Hey, it's nearly one. I'm hungry. There's a great fish and chip spot up ahead. Wanna run in there for lunch?"

"Ah, yes, that sounds good."

"Okay. And I'm buying. You've been picking up my lunch tab for weeks."

Alex grinned. "Right. I guess it's your turn."

They had lunch overlooking the water. Delicious food, a glass of wine. They debriefed the encounter. Ben learned about book club books. Poor quality paper and boards. Once you've handled a few, it's obvious.

Alex figured they might have some pricey kid picture books in the stash. And Agathas always sell, so they did well under the circumstances.

Alex learned she would never go on one of these scouting trips into a stranger's home alone. You never know. Ben told her he'd be glad to ride along. Maybe next time he would carry a small weapon. There are nutcases everywhere.

The store was humming along when they got back. Both Serena and Rishi were glad to see them. They needed lunch. Ben stacked the boxes for Ellie. Alex asked him to take the box with the books in the slipcases to the loft. She would decide on their prices. She figured she underpaid for those, but the guy didn't ask for a breakdown. His loss.

Alex let brother and sister have lunch together. They earned it. She and Ben could handle things. It had been an interesting day so far. Good lunch too. She had forgotten how fun it is to go to lunch with colleagues occasionally. She might work in some coffees and lunches with the rest of the gang.

That night Alex took a look at the books from the kid. Nice books. It looked like they had never been read. Old titles like All Quiet on the Western Front, the Moon and Six Pence, and Forever Amber.

The last slipcase book had been hollowed out. She opened it. A wad of cash that looked like old bills. Somebody's forgotten stash of emergency money. Several hundred dollars. Receipts, letters, and a spare key. A birthday card, some postcards. A cookie recipe.

Alex decided to call Murf. Maybe she'd help put a price on the slipcase books. She looked at the atlases. Perhaps she'd ask about those too.

Days later, Ellie was still working on the last load. She was excited. She'd been taking her time with the kids' books.

"Look at this one, Alex. The value is ninety-five dollars. The Mouse. It's not worn, and it has gorgeous illustrations. A first. Wow!"

Alex loved seeing Ellie so excited about books. "That's a real find, my dear. We'll have to add children's books to our collectible shelf."

Ellie smiled, "Okay, and there are others too. Oh, I meant to ask you, is it okay if I read those Agatha Christie books? She's my favorite."

"Of course. Why don't you pick up a handful? Your choice. We'll make it a gift. You deserve a bonus. This has been a huge job."

Ellie was thrilled. She quickly picked out a few. Alex nodded. "Take them off the inventory. They are yours."

Alex adored Ellie. She was a natural in the store. She loved her work and hanging around with everybody. She was intelligent and resourceful. A great employee.

The store looked so pretty by the last week of November. Serena and Ellie outdid themselves. They enlisted Ben to get out the ladder and hold it so they could reach the tall branches of the enormous tree they were decorating for the holidays.

The store was hosting several Christmas parties and a wedding. It was essentially the same party over and over. But the guests didn't know that as long as the staff kept things fresh and lively. So, no slip-ups. Make sure everybody was having fun.

Didn't everybody love bookstores at Christmas? They did their best to provide little surprises at the register for last-minute shopping. Everything they set out was purchased. Customers were eager to bring a piece of bookstore magic into their homes.

Their big winner was a candle called the Scent of a Bookstore. A specialty candlemaker had come in and offered to create a one-of-a-kind candle for them. Bookstore-scented candles were a hit. Also, chocolate in many forms, note pads, postcards of the bookstore inside and out, pens, journals, markers, and bookmarks all went out the door.

It was bound to happen. The last Christmas party of the year went out of control. Somebody brought in something. Or maybe several things, and a couple guys got toasted and started fighting. Caught the staff off guard. This wasn't supposed to happen.

Rishi and Ben glanced at each other and nodded. They quickly moved in. Ben grabbed one big guy by the arm and twisted it behind his back, cop style. Rishi grabbed the other guy.

Ben said, "We're going outside. I'll accidentally break your arm if you don't go quietly."

Ethan ran and opened the door. Then he turned to the embarrassed guests and found the person who claimed to be in charge.

The guest host stepped up, "I'm so sorry this happened. They are a couple of hotheads. This isn't the first time."

Ethan said, "You've got two choices. Somebody needs to drive those two home, or we have to call the police."

The group looked around. Nobody volunteered.

"Okay, then, the police will be on their way."

Alex grabbed her phone and made the call. Outside, the guys were so out of it that they could barely stand up. So Ben let them sit. They were still yelling at each other when the cops rolled up and took over. Rishi explained what happened. The cops loaded them up and took off.

Back inside, the rest of the group was relieved. And so sorry. Alex looked carefully around the room. Knocked-over chairs had been righted. Spilled food and drinks were wiped up. The host pleaded that they let them continue. They hadn't chosen their gifts for each other yet.

Alex said okay, secretly delighted. Good outcome. The group breathed a communal sigh of relief. It took them a few minutes to return to the party atmosphere, but they sorted things out and then hit the bookshelves. Giggling was heard, furtive looks, sneaking around. They found the party again. And they found gifts, the cash register rang, and the gift wrapping went into high gear.

At the door, as the goodbyes were underway, the host again apologized and handed Alex an extra two hundred for the two men who handled things so quickly. He was impressed. It might have been a lot worse.

When the last guests had left, the gang cheered and breathed their own sigh.

"So," Alex said, "you guys have a contingency plan already in place, huh?"

Rishi grinned. "Yes, ma'am, Ben thought it up, just in case. It worked perfectly. We practiced the moves and everything."

Alex turned to Ben. He shrugged his shoulders. "I took a defensive protection course. The Toledo police taught it. I didn't think these little parties would get out of hand. But you never know. We knew what to do."

Everybody cheered.

CHAPTER 8

The week before Christmas was a bookstore madhouse. Alex now had a much better understanding of the term: Black Friday. It was the time of year when businesses started making profits. That was definitely the case for Seaside Books. Customers were waiting for the doors to open. Alex had no idea that books could be such a big draw.

So it was all hands whenever possible. They opened earlier and stayed open longer. Staff was working overtime nearly every day. They did several kid parties while the store was open. Ellie worked those parties as hostess with Serena. Lots of noise and cookie crumbs and spilled drinks, but that was easily remedied. The kids acted out stories wearing masks. Moms helped with that. They played duck, duck goose, and sang songs. After an hour, moms and kids picked out gift books for their friends. Moms were delighted. The kids were happy. And then they left, making everybody else very happy.

There were book stacks everywhere. Dwindling piles of bestsellers, the Christmas cards were well thumbed and nearly gone. The calendars, journals, cookbooks, and children's read-along books were in disarray. The store was joyously messy with anticipation of the big day.

Christmas Eve finally arrived. They closed the store at noon. It was time for their own party. Alex had contacted a catering service with a mobile kitchen to prepare lunch for them. They dragged the table from the stage down to the front of the store by the tree.

The caterers were there. The table was set, and lunch appeared. Crab salad, a delicious lasagna, and sparkling wine. A layer cake for dessert. They were all hungry and anxious to sit down together and celebrate. When the lunch was over, the caterers quickly cleaned up and left.

The staff had each brought a group gift of something else. 'No books' had been the Christmas party theme. So they opened their gifts with howls of laughter. Sore feet seemed to be a popular concept. Fuzzy slippers, foot lotion, and socks that looked like animals. It was hilarious. Then Alex handed out the bonus checks. They had earned them. The store would be closed until the 26th. Expect another big day. Until then, go home and enjoy the holiday.

Everybody hugged, wished each other Merry Christmas and headed for the door. Family awaited them. Everybody except Alex and Ben.

"Oh, Ben, I forgot. You're alone too." She smiled, "Familiar territory for me. What's left of my family is miles away, and distant in other ways too. You?"

"Yes, the same. We never had kids. My parents are gone. I, too, have distant relatives. I didn't even get cards this year. But I think it's my fault. I might have forgotten to let them know my new address. Ah, well.

They sat there for a while, admiring the tree, now bare of its gifts, looking like Christmas past. Alex picked up an open bottle of wine and gestured to him with her eyes.

"Yes, thank you. I'd love some more wine."

The store opened on the 26th at eleven. The staff had showed up an hour earlier and hustled to make things presentable. Store policy was credit only for returned books with receipts. They did a brisk business in returns, which went onto store carts for reshelving. Christmas items sold for half off. They left the store quickly, along with many credit sales, often accompanied by a little additional cash spent. A sale table had been arranged, a bookstore tradition.

Ben and Alex were somewhat shy with each other. Ben had spent the night with Alex and most of the next day in her cozy loft. They had become lovers, a surprise to both of them.

It hadn't been planned or thought of until the second glass of wine. But then, the ah-hah moment. Suddenly, it seemed to make sense.

Two lonely middle-aged people who liked each other had been working together for months. Could they? Should they? Why not? Nothing to lose, everything to gain.

They walked out into the rain, a steady drenching winter rain. By the time they reached the top of the stairs, the entrance to her loft, they had kissed several times, familiar kisses. They had both been there before.

The cats looked at Ben when he walked through the door and scattered. Their Christmas was ruined. It was a different experience for Ben and Alex. They had a surprisingly wonderful Christmas. They found out they were just a few years apart in age. He was younger than Alex thought. She was a bit older than Ben thought. Ah, isn't that nice? Age mates.

They flirted and danced together. They scrounged through the refrigerator for some dinner. There was plenty of time. A lifetime of time. They tried to watch a movie together. They found they couldn't concentrate on it. So they said goodnight to the tv and went off to bed together. He left the next afternoon late.

"See you in the morning. Yes. Merry Christmas.

Yes."

There was no store policy about fraternizing. Alex would have given it some thought if it had come up. It hadn't because all of her employees were related. She hadn't realized how blessed she was for that.

But now she had to think about it. Until further notice, she and Ben would not admit they had a thing going on. That would lead to gossip, giggling, and who knew what else. The business should come first.

The store's official year end was January 31. Close the books and see where she stood. She needed to talk to Darlene. That was the thorniest piece of unfinished business. They would have an arbitrator figure out where they stood financially. Alex thought she would end up being the sole proprietor.

Darlene had become more distant over time. When Alex suggested she come to the store, she either declined outright or made excuses. At first Alex was dismayed and upset. But then it became clear that what she had gone through with the baby and Tru had hit her pretty hard. She was coping, but there just wasn't room for the bookstore. So Alex took it in stride. She was doing fine. Learning how to run a store had been interesting and unsettling. New territory. But she did it. .She was good at it. Maybe even better since she didn't have to compromise with a partner.

So now her second year was beginning. She had new goals for the store, possible new revenue streams, and a great staff. And even though she could hardly believe it, she had a man in her life. A good man. She had given up hope that she would ever have a partner. But now, a new year and many new possibilities.

January was the month of sales as businesses tried to slim down inventory for tax reasons. Christmas had given them a head start. Now they were focusing on old inventory, marking it down, and hoping to sell it. It was a struggle to decide just which books needed to be sold off cheaply.

Ethan had an idea. Appeal to the guilty reader. They created a table of 'books I never finished reading.' They pulled the classics off the shelves and piled them up.

"Start the new year right. Finish that book". The table got lots of laughs and some sales.

Travel books were showcased. Also DIYs, the subject of many New Year's resolutions. Customers liked the sense of humor throughout the store.

Then the winter blues set in. The unending rain and wind were depressing. The gray skies, gray sand, and even gray waves contributed to foul moods, sour looks, and vile dispositions. Customers dwindled.

Does anybody get married in January? The parties came to a halt. Business slowed down. Ethan could concentrate on his classes. He was nearly finished with his AA at the community college. Not too interested in going on at the moment. He and Ellie would continue with the same schedule. Serena's events were slow too. Rishi was on hand. Alex would rework their schedules, but they wouldn't lose many hours.

Alex was considering some minor renovations to the store. She definitely wanted an inside stairway and a small private office. A better break room. Another cash register. There were several things they could do to use the space more efficiently. Now was the time for that. She called the contractor and a designer.

Ben stayed on. Alex wanted to do more book scouting of estates and private sales. She checked out some listings and was following up on them. It was the slow time for the real estate market, but winter decluttering would start soon.

Murf called. She was driving over the following Monday. She could drop in and look at the books. Maybe give Alex some tips on estate sales. They could have lunch too. A date.

Ben was happy not to get laid off. He would make himself useful by checking out the local thrift stores for books. A good idea. Also, the store needed to be staffed, even if there were only a few customers. Alex preferred two booksellers on hand at all times, if possible. Inventory updates were due at the end of the month. They could start on them soon.

She talked to Ethan and Rishi about young people their age. The one group who never seemed to show up. They agreed.

"They live on another planet, a strange world. No interest in books." The unreachables, as far as Ethan and Rishi were concerned. They just weren't interested in books.

Ben brought in a few boxes of books from his first run. He did well. He definitely knew which books the store would take. He was reimbursed. The books would be inventoried in February when the new fiscal year arrived.

Murf valued the old books between fifty to one hundred each. The slipcases were only valuable as protection. Some collectors liked them. It's the dust jacket that makes the difference. She showed Alex the sites she used to derive rare book values. They talked about estates. Sometimes there were just too many books for one store. Call her if she had questions.

Alex and Ben were seeing each other, but it was hard to find time. He had an apartment a few blocks away, but he didn't want her walking over there at night. That was one of Seaside's black marks, muggers. So she drove and parked in the space reserved for guests. If she had to park on the street, call and he'd come get her. No nonsense.

Alex said, "You know, you act more like a cop than an accountant."

Ben laughed but didn't say anything. Alex figured she was right.

It turned out Ben liked to cook. Excellent, because Alex didn't. He'd fix something nice for dinner, they would watch a little tv, and so forth. Then he'd walk her to the car. Ben stayed with Alex on Sunday nights. He could sleep over and not risk being caught. It was working. They enjoyed each other's company. Too bad they were both working so hard. They could be off traveling together if they were retired.

Alex got an invitation to an estate sale preview. She and Ben showed up early. A big house overlooking the beach at the far end of the prom. The crew of sales facilitators wandered around helping previewers. The whole place was a giant store, the family treasures displayed with prices on everything except the books. They were in the library.

Alex whispered to Ben, "Holy crap. I have no idea where to start."

It was one of those showcase libraries, leather volumes, floor to ceiling. Behind glass. All old, all obscure titles. There was nothing in this room that interested them.

Alex called over a seller and explained that her store sold current fiction. "Are there other books in the house besides this formal room?"

The seller said, "Pretty daunting, right?" Alex nodded.

She showed them to another library. This one was way more familiar. She asked if they could go through the books. The answer was not shocking. They were selling this collection as a lot. Give them a bid. If it was acceptable, they could take them today. She left.

Alex started looking through the books, some were in good shape, others should have been tossed or donated. They wanted the buyers to do the dirty work.

Ben started on one side, Alex on the other, doing a rough count of how many they could actually use. They came to the same conclusion. Not interested. Too much work hauling them off and then figuring out what to do with the trash.

They told the seller the bad news. Too many

books that they couldn't use. She said, "Wait here a second." She came back with another woman who looked somewhat frazzled.

The woman said, "What gives with you folks? Nobody is interested in any of the books. You are the third pair through here."

Alex explained that they worked on a tight budget. It would be too costly to haul all of these books to their store, go through them, and then have to make a dump run. Most of the books weren't in good condition. Sorry.

She fumed for a few minutes and then asked, "What would you give for the books you could use?"

Ben and Alex conferred. They decided on $150 for about a third of the books. That was slightly more than Got Junk would charge to haul them away.

She rolled her eyes and fumed some more. Then said, "Take what you want for $150." The woman beside her nodded. "You have to take them now."

Ben got the boxes, and they started packing up. It was interesting to see how the owner had mistreated the books. Alex wondered why they wanted all those leather-bound books hanging around when they obviously weren't collectors. She suspected those were junk too. So much to learn.

Back on the street, they laughed. Once again they had pissed off the seller. Only this time Ben didn't even once feel the need to pull a gun. Hilarious.

They ate at the same place and returned to the store with inventory for the new year.

Darlene was there when they pulled in. Ben unloaded while they chatted. Dar was alone and looked exhausted. They went over to Starbucks to talk.

"So Alex," she started, "I hear you did quite well this year. Congratulations."

"Well, it's a matter of opinion. Where did you hear that?"

"Oh, Tru mentioned it. He heard it somewhere."

Alex laughed. "Tru! He's no businessman. Here's what I did last year. I made payroll, I paid the bills. I still haven't taken a salary or even a draw from the business. When I pull the records together, my out-of-pocket expenses will eat up any profit I might have made. Do you call that doing quite well?"

"Jeez, you don't have to get so angry. It was just gossip."

"Darlene, you could have come in any time to find out how we're doing. You were not interested. So, why now?"

"Well, I'm not happy with the way the arbitration is going. That's all. I think I'm getting jerked around."

"Well, guess what? I'm not going to have that discussion with you. That's why we hired help. You know, objective professionals figuring things out for us."

"Tru thinks you probably paid them off!"

"What? Tru again. Are you still seeing him?" Alex was angry now.

Darlene growled, "He is the father of our baby girl. He's entitled to an opinion."

"Not about the bookstore, he isn't. That turd. He's a jerk, Darlene. By the way, I thought you referred to him as the sperm donor. He's nothing but a sperm donor, a gold-plated jerk, and a troublemaker."

She started crying. "I'm pregnant again."

CHAPTER 9

What was Darlene thinking?

After hearing her confession, Alex just said "congratulations" and walked out. She would do her best to ignore it all: the Tru part, the arbitration part, and the baby part. She had nothing to say, to add, to suggest, or to critique. Darlene always had a hard time making decisions. Now this. She was living her life. You go, girl.

Then the arbitration decision came in. Alex had to pay Darlene one fifty for the business and fifty for the house to reimburse her for renovation expenses. Alex now owned the business and her loft. She didn't have to hand over any future profits, nothing. And it was a binding decision, agreed to from the start of negotiations.

It had been a complicated deal because they entered the thing as friends, not as business associates. The arbitrators had to sift through some unusual problems. Alex wouldn't make that mistake again.

And then there was Covid, still hanging around.

Folks didn't want to wear masks, so there were outbreaks, but mild cases. At various times the staff would mask up, especially at the register. Alex told Ellie to stay in the back and limit her customer interaction. She agreed. The bottom line, it affected the bookstore business.

So Alex decided to close the store for a couple weeks while that renovation was underway. It wouldn't take long. The staircase was just carpentry and painting. A narrow one in the back. The other work wasn't structural either. Just a few walls, some added electrical outlets and paint. The contractor thought they could complete it in a month.

The staff would take turns being on hand when the workers were there so Alex and Ben could sneak off on a vacation. They decided to go south to Puerto Vallarta for a couple of weeks. It sounded dreamy and romantic to Alex. No books.

Nobody officially knew that Alex and Ben were seeing each other outside of work, but it was becoming rather apparent. Nobody said anything negative. Two nice people meet in a bookstore. Why not?

Puerto Vallarta was calling, except that Ben couldn't leave the country. What? He was on the No Fly list. Even he didn't know it. When they tried to get their tickets, his name was flagged.

"Well, son of a bitch." Ben had to fess up. "Yes, you are right." He was an ex-cop.

Alex felt smug and laughed. "That was a very poor impersonation of an accountant. You never mentioned balance sheets or profit and loss statements once. A dead giveaway."

He grinned. "That bad, huh? Yeah, I'm a retired cop, detective, actually. I was working a big case, narcotics. Some big shots got mad and threatened me. Most of them are in prison now. Headquarters decided I might be in danger. Since I was close to retirement, they worked things out so I could escape. Just go find some small town and retire. Change my name to make me hard to find. That's what I've done. Not a big deal.

"I'm gonna make some calls. Find out why I can't leave the country. This sucks." He was surprised.

Alex thought about it. Maybe they didn't need to fight that battle right now. There were other choices. Perhaps they could drive to Palm Springs?

Ben said, "A road trip? Not a bad idea, but it's a crumby time of year for driving long distances."

Alex was remembering the hurried coastal drive on the way to Seaside. "What about we drive down the coast, stop often, poke around. The sights are breathtaking."

"I like that idea. Take it slow. Check out the little towns. Maybe find us a cozy beach house getaway. That sounds good to me."

So they repacked their bags for cold weather. She took the cats to the local pet hotel, where the owners guaranteed her little ones would be well cared for. And they took off. The rain had stopped momentarily. They were between storms, so it was pleasant driving.

They didn't get far. About twenty-five miles down the road, they found Manzanita, a very small town on a river. Gorgeous views. They picked a place for lunch, friendly waiters wondering if they were here for the king tide.

Ben looked at Alex, who shrugged, "Maybe we are." They located a small cabin close by and checked in. Bought some groceries and decided to stay a few days. The king tide occurred the next day, booming waves close to the road. They watched the big waves crashing into the rocks. Spectacular!

Later they strolled the beach, watching out for sneaker waves. A popular beach. They weren't alone. They found tourist info online. Bears in the local state park. That might be fun. A cute little town with good restaurants.

Their cabin turned out to be just as cozy as advertised. It was snug with a gas fireplace, a small modern kitchen, and a comfy bed for two. Updated bath. Good sprawling on the couch. Tourist rates. They didn't blink. Ben insisted on paying.

They spent the evening talking about his career as a cop. And how it ended. He might have fought for his job if his wife hadn't been so ill. He was going to take a leave anyhow to care for her. So it ended badly. His wife lasted about six months after he retired. His boss told him they were worried that he'd be gunned down on the street. Leave the state and change your name, just in case. Don't come back. So that's what he did. He wasn't one bit worried, never looked over his shoulder, and he liked his new name. She smiled. She did too.

His mood was infectious. He asked her about Darlene. He had heard about her, the absent partner, but he'd never met her. She told him the details. Her recent conversation with Darlene was still playing in the background, irritating her whenever she thought about it.

Ben asked, "So what's with this Tru guy? He sounds like an angry loser. What's that about? He doesn't have any interest in the store, right?"

"None whatsoever. We don't hit it off. I refer to him as the sperm donor."

He laughed. Then he thought for a minute. "Does

he wear cowboy clothes, sort of short, good-looking, eyes on the women?"

"Yup. That's a good description of him. You've seen him?"

"Uh-huh. He hangs around the Starbucks. I thought he was watching Rishi the other day. Is Tru gay or something?"

"No, I don't think so. He has a lot of problems and keeps looking for more. He must be out of work again."

Ben added, "I saw him a few days ago with a woman. I think she was crying. Dark hair, long, wearing a big coat. Fidgeting. Could that have been Darlene?"

"Nope. Darlene has curly red hair. She's short, cute smile. Glasses."

Ben watched people closely. A cop thing.

Alex could tell he was mulling things over. Putting puzzle pieces together, but the pieces all fit different puzzles as far as she was concerned.

She explained, "Umm, that's Tru's Starbucks. You know how people are about Starbucks? They usually go to the same one. That's where Darlene met Tru."

Ben nodded, not convinced. "If he's out of work, what's he doing in Starbucks all the time? It isn't cheap. A coffee and a pastry is about $7 these days. That's a lot day after day for us working stiffs."

"Tell me about it."

They stayed for a week, finding enough to amuse them during the day, and evenings spent making dinner, watching a little tv, and sleeping in.

Next they drove down to Newport. It was a wealthy town, larger than Manzanita, with lots of mansions. They found another cabin on the beach, so they decided to just bunk there for the last week. They visited the aquarium and both lighthouses and then wandered through town. They spotted several thrift stores, so they did a book check. They ended up with a box of good ones. No Antique Roadshow treasures. But it was fun to be on the hunt again.

On their last night they found the most romantic dinner house. They were still enjoying each other's company even more after two weeks. Neither of them wanted this vacation to end. It was time to talk about the next step in their relationship since it was becoming evident that they were a good match.

They had a long leisurely dinner, their last meal before heading back. Ben was the realist. He brought up the subject.

"So Alex, what's next for us? I've enjoyed being with you like this. No kidding. It's been more than fun."

Alex was quiet. Thoughtful. "I know. This has been such a pleasant getaway. Just what I needed. But life just seems so complicated right now. I don't know what we do next." she said.

"The bookstore, right?"

"Yes. Honestly, I'm not sure how long I want to own a bookstore. I went into it with a partner, thinking we could share the work. Also, not realizing how incredibly time-consuming it would be. Frankly, it hasn't been all that rewarding, and I'm not talking about money here. I've been too busy even to think straight most of the time. If it weren't for you guys, it would be a complete failure. I've made payroll and paid the bills. Apparently, that's a success in the book business. I should be celebrating. But all I can think of is can I do it again next year?"

Ben was listening carefully. "Huh. I had no idea you've been under so much pressure. I know nothing about the business end of owning a bookstore. All I know is that I'm having a great time. I love my job."

"Ah, that's good to know. Work environment is everything. I don't think I've ever really loved any job. But I wouldn't have met you if I was still at my old job. So there's that."

"Me neither. I desperately needed something to

do. I've been here for over a year. When I chose Seaside to settle down, I didn't realize that tourist towns are different from other places. Most of the work here supports tourism. Service work. It's kind of a two-tiered economy. Tourists with money to spend on recreation on one hand, and the local folks working low-paid jobs to support them.

"Being a retiree puts me in a different category. Some retirees are here because it's cheaper to live here than home. So they hunker down, pinch pennies, and make the social security check go farther. Others with more money can take advantage of the area's nice restaurants, trendy shops, cheap housing, and cheap living. The problem is that retirees are sort of out of place with the other locals. It's awkward."

Ben looked at Alex and took her hand across the table.

"Sorry, a long explanation to say I was bored and lonely. I was thinking I would have to look for another place to live. Then I saw the sign in the window and you."

Alex felt tears. She tried to wipe them away. "I had convinced myself that I was just destined to be lonely. You took me by surprise."

Ben nodded. "Same here. We've found each other. I want to spend the rest of my life with you."

Alex just nodded, tears again.

Ben continued, "You know, I never thought I'd ever say this again, but here goes. Alex, will you marry me?"

He reached into his pocket and pulled out a ring box. Handed it to Alex. She was crying now, her hands shaking and toying with the box.

"Open it, Alex. Just open it and say yes."

She did. It was a beautiful engagement ring. It made her gasp. Nobody had ever given her such a gift or spoken those words to her. She smiled through her tears, and he placed the ring on her finger.

"Yes, Ben, I will marry you."

He was in tears too. "There's another proposal I'd like to make. How about I become your business partner too? Let's find an attorney and do it right. Figure out what the business is worth and the loft, and I'll pay you half. It seems like the only fair thing to do. We become business partners first, and then we get married.

"I'll take on half of the load, give you some breathing room. We'll run the store for a while and see how it goes. When we get tired of it, we sell it. And go become full-time retirees together."

"Wow, that's quite an offer. But you know, it

makes sense. I like it. We sink or swim together, right? Partners."

"Yeah. Marrying you is one thing, but the store is a complication. I wouldn't want people to talk about me as some freeloader who married Alex and her bookstore. Cops don't do that."

"Yes, that's the awkward part. I guess technically, you'd own half of it anyhow if we got married. I'm not sure about Oregon law. We'll get the lawyers to explain it."

"Yup. Let's get that part straightened out first. Money changing hands. So we're proper partners. Then we get married."

"Good idea, Ben."

When they returned, the renovation work was nearly finished and ahead of schedule. It looked great. The stairs were perfect and blended in, both upstairs and downstairs. A door that locked in the loft. Open stairs in the back. Easy access. A sign would say 'Private."

The other rooms were an improvement too. A better break room and a small office. They did lose floor space for books, but it was worth it.

Alex called a pizza meeting as soon as they got home. The staff needed to hear the news. Significant changes were coming. They applauded the happy couple. They wanted the wedding ceremony to be at the bookstore, of course.

Then the big news. Ben was Alex's business partner. She laughed. "Get this: that means he goes off payroll, but to make up for it, he will work longer hours."

Everybody laughed.

"So for you all, that means we can hire another employee. We will be rearranging the whole store, so we need help. If you know somebody who will fit right in, tell them there's an opening."

Ben chimed in. Alex will continue to be the boss, I'm an employee, same as always. So no questioning decisions. My specialty will be bookstore safety and security. The rest of the time, I'm a bookseller.

The pizza was delicious, the wine and the conversations were bright. They knew their jobs were secure if they wanted to stay on. A happy new year to look forward to. Things to think about.

The grand reopening was publicized. The crew wore hard hats and painter aprons. They got some laughs. They set up book sale tables outside on sawhorses. All home improvement books were half off. Store information bookmarks were printed on paint chip cards. Store decor was old tools that they rounded up from garage sales. They ended up selling most of them. They got freebie buckets from hardware stores that they used as carry-out bags. They kept it up for a week. Each day they got more customers.

At the next Tuesday night meeting, the marketing idea was celebrated. Alex was especially pleased. It had been fun and profitable.

CHAPTER 10

Alex was still surprised that she was wearing an engagement ring. Of course, it was the natural progression of their relationship. Still, she had been unprepared for the moment he proposed to her. She wasn't exactly having second thoughts. She was just uneasy. Perhaps it was just nerves. They got along so well.

Ben wasn't having second thoughts at all. He moved in, bringing little from his apartment, so his move wasn't intrusive. He got rid of what he didn't need. And he took over kitchen duties, including grocery shopping and clean-up.

Even the cats were getting used to Ben. One night, one of them crawled into Ben's lap as they watched tv. That settled it for Alex.

Ben had planned how to earn the cats' affection. He studied the cat food aisle in Safeway like a good detective. Treats took up as many shelves as canned food, which would be a separate investigation. Broth-like goodies in envelopes appeared to be the rage. 'Delights' were a huge hit in the mornings. And 'Broths' at bedtime. Fancy Feast seafood at noon. After a couple of weeks, the cats were in the kitchen with him all the time.

But the thing that sealed the deal was laser red-dot playtime. The two cats chased around like crazy. They couldn't get enough. After a few red-dot sessions, Ben owned the cats.

Alex and Ben went to the lawyers and told them their plan. Ben's buy-in was being implemented. Once they figured out what the bookstore was worth, Ben wrote a check and bought half. They were co-owners.

Spring rain showed up. There had been grumbling throughout the state about the drought conditions devastating the forests, especially in the central Cascades. It was a truly dire situation and it was due to climate change.

Oregon forests are vital for the health of the planet. The lack of sufficient rain was causing the trees to die. When these otherwise healthy trees die, they turn red. So agencies were sending planes to fly over miles and miles of Oregon forests to monitor the damage. Vast swathes of trees had turned red. It was a shocking event to see how many trees were affected. So Oregon was praying that the drought would lift.

By April the bookstore was awash in nature books. Since the causes and effects of climate change were now clearly stated, the issue was on everybody's mind. Humans need to change. So the store went all out. They created an extensive window display of animal picture books. Animals depend on a stable climate, just like humans do. The other big front window was devoted to severe environmental problems, the politics of nature.

That's when the hate mail began in earnest. Mail from the general public was a foreign thing to the bookstore. Aside from bills and book catalogs, nobody sends mail to bookstores. Personal, handwritten letters, snail mail letters showed up. Ugly letters with simple messages:

American jobs are for Americans, not Indians

Lesbians go home

Climate change is a hoax

Accidents happen to bad people

America First

Californians go home

Ethan opened the mail as part of his daily routine. He was shocked when he saw the ugly letters. He showed them to everybody as they came in. Ben didn't like them. They kept them in a file. Once they began to identify the letters, Ben told Ethan to leave them unopened. Just handle the envelopes by the edges and put them in the file. If the bookstore had any incidents, they would turn them over to the cops.

Then an anti-environmental group started flooding their Facebook page with the same stuff. They had to turn off the comments. Facebook was no help with any other suggestions. Yelp reviews turned ugly. They made both Ben and Alex uneasy. Seaside residents and tourists ignored them.

After a few months with no attempts to respond to the threats by the bookstore, the letter writer ran out of hate and slowed it down until April, when the Earth Day celebrations began.

The bookstore's involvement with climate change didn't sit well with the gun-toting, maga-hatted right-wing fringe element. Alex awoke one morning early to see a bunch of pot-bellied old guys milling around in front of the store carrying AR15s and sipping McDonald's senior-sized coffees.

She woke Ben, who took one look and got dressed in a hurry. He was on the phone about a minute later with the police department. Yes, he understood that peaceful protests were legal. This didn't look peaceful to Ben. It looked like one of those so-called maga rallies where armed militias try to intimidate folks from going into certain businesses. The cops were on the way.

Next, Ben called the Seaside and Astoria

newspapers and local tv news stations and reported an armed militia outside his store. He figured the media would be at the store soon and would start filming immediately. Armed maga-hatted hate groups who want to threaten folks aren't keen on "the fake news" showing up.

He went downstairs, turned on the front bookstore lights, opened the door, and went outside alone. The first thing he noticed was somebody fixing to throw something through the window.

He yelled, "Hey! Don't do that!"

The guy dropped the rock and moved off.

"Who's in charge here?" Ben boomed out to the crowd.

One big old guy came up to Ben and said. "Who wants to know?"

"I do. I'm the owner, and I'd like to know why strange men with assault rifles are at my door."

The guy deflected the question and said, "Yer probly lyin'. Some old lesbo owns this place."

Ben answered, "Take your ugly bigotry somewhere else. That creep over there just tried to throw a rock through the window. You are yelling insults. Just who do you think you are?"

Potbelly said, "It's still a free country, last I heard."

"You're not free to damage buildings and scare strangers, yell insults, and threaten folks with guns. You are gonna find that out soon enough."

They heard the sirens. The cops were on their way. Some of the group started scattering. Probably the ones who were out on bail from their last dust-up. This quiet, family-oriented little beach town was having a problem. Ben hoped the cops had figured out how to handle these idiots. He didn't have a clue other than to shine as many lights as possible on them and hope they said something stupid enough to land themselves in jail.

He could feel his gun tucked into his belt. It gave him no feeling of security. He only had one plan. He wanted to dangle enough bait in front of Potbelly to trip him up in front of the cop. Get him to do or say something stupid enough to get arrested.

"Why'd you call the cops, you dumb ass? We ain't done nothing yet."

Ben chuckled. "Sheriff's on his way too, just in case."

The guy behind him swore under his breath and peeled off.

"Damn it to hell. You got no business doing that. Your lefty ass store ain't even open yet."

"That's nothing," Ben said, "The local news will be here soon with the cameras, so get your best smile ready. Be prepared to tell the world what you're up to this fine morning. Remember that half your group scattered when they heard the sirens. The Oregonian helicopter is about half an hour out."

At that point, an impatient hothead fired off his weapon straight into the air. His frustration with the slowness of the rally just got to him. The burst emptied his gun. All his pals started yelling at him and running for cover. A few Starbucks patrons standing under a metal roof watched the whole thing, laughing. The spent bullets began falling on the rioters. One of the gang was struck in the head and fell to the ground. Others were hurt too.

That's when the cops showed up. They had heard the shots fired just as they pulled up. Perfect timing. They ran in with weapons drawn, yelling, "Throw down your guns!"

Ben backed into the doorway to watch. Amused. He loved watching the cops in situations like this one. Shots had been fired. There were bad guys out there to take down. Whoever had fired off his rifle had given the cops precisely what they needed to stop this little show.

The magas were identified easily by their hats, their ARs, their ammo belts, and of course, their angry looks and pot bellies. This wasn't their first rally in Seaside. So the cops knew them by name, even though most didn't live in Seaside.

The cops had a field day. After all the weapons were rounded up, they were told to sit down with their hands on their heads. Then the paramedics came through and gave first aid to those hit by falling debris. Several went off to the hospital. The shooter was arrested and placed in handcuffs, yelling 'fascist pigs' as they dragged him off. There were dozens of witnesses to his stupidity. He had injured a handful of people.

Soon the local news film crew were on the ground filming everything. Even the cops were having fun this time. It was a righteous takedown. For once. They let the film crew and reporters do their work. Once the cops had things in hand and the leaders corralled, two cops came into the store to talk to Ben and Alex.

When Ben started talking, they realized it would take a while, so they gathered around the table. Ben began by reciting what had happened before they showed up. They listened and took notes. Alex mentioned the incident in the store from the previous year. Then Ethan handed over the file of letters.

Alex sent Rishi to Starbucks for coffee and pastries. Everybody was hungry so they dug in. Then they went back to the rest of the story.

When the cops were finished, Alex and Ben invited the reporters in for another sit-down. They went over the same story. Ben showed the reporters and the film crew the letters. They took photos.

They also filmed Ben telling the story. Then they photographed the booksellers, all members of the well-liked local Patel family. They weren't illegal immigrants. The family had lived in Seaside for years, all tax-paying outstanding citizens. Finally, they took photos of the store's front windows as Ben talked about its commitment to social issues of the day.

The incident was winding down. Things were returning to normal. Another day at the store could begin. Many customers, sympathetic store patrons, carried out plenty of books that day. It had been exciting from start to finish.

"See what I mean," Alex said, as she put her feet up and accepted a glass of wine, "You just never know what's gonna happen next. I'm exhausted."

Ben grinned. He was exhilarated. "But that was so much fun, Alex," he raved. "It was brilliant. After that jerk shot off his gun, the whole day changed. I couldn't have dreamed up a better end for those haters."

He told her how scared he was when he confronted the potbellied leader in front of the store. He was trying to think of something he could do that would rile him up. He wanted to give the cops some reason to break up the incident. So Ben was trying to goad the old geezer into doing something stupid.

Instead, another angry old dude became impatient, blew a gasket, and started shooting into the air. Straight up into the clouds. What an idiot. He unloaded every bullet, which then rained down on them. Perfect timing. That's when the cops showed up.

Ben went on and on. Then they turned on the news and watched a replay of it. The local news loved the story. They went into great detail. Even the police got into it, happy to deal a blow to that toxic group. They had been harassing the town for way too long. Now they are all facing charges.

"Ben, do you think they'll come back?" Alex was worried sick. The whole day had been an ordeal, as far as she was concerned.

"I don't know. I wonder about that too. My guess is they are all scared. Why do folks do crap like that? What's in it for them? I wonder if somebody pays them. Somebody with lots of money, some climate change denier? I don't get the point of denying climate change. Or anything these hate groups claim to believe. It's just so puzzling."

"And why us? We're a small business selling used books, not some big-time outfit that can make a lot of noise."

Ben agreed. It just didn't make sense. "Ya know, muggers walking around holding people up, stealing their cash, that I understand. But militias, a complete mystery."

"But us, Ben. What about us?"

"Yeah, us, the store, and the kids who run it. What about us? I think we're okay. They're bullies, basically. They want us to close up, I guess. Hate groups are puzzling. They aren't willing to go to jail for their beliefs. So that's the deterrent. They do something idiotic, and off they go.

"The cops will let most of them off. There are not enough broken laws to hold them on unless they have outstanding warrants or were out on bail. Even bench warrants for parking tickets would hold them for a while. They have expensive guns, so I guess they have bail money. We gotta watch our backs for a while. The cops said they'll patrol often. And they will make calls from us a priority. Maybe some of that crazy bunch will have enough sense to back off."

"Ben, I'm hearing a lot of cop talk. I hope you are right. If anything happens to the staff, I can't live with myself. That's what I'm thinking about.

Let's have a staff meeting in the morning. See what they are thinking."

The meeting restored Alex's faith in human beings. They made it a special meeting with breakfast items, coffee and orange juice. The six of them hashed it out. Even Ellie was there.

Alex was the most scared. Even the Patel parents weren't as alarmed as Alex. They brushed it off. School shootings were more worrisome. They came up with two ideas.

First, hire another staff member. A big guy, a nice guy, but white, so he wouldn't antagonize the haters. Somebody who likes books, maybe a young retiree, like Ben. Full time. Maybe ex-cop or FBI. They were dreaming. But somebody who would like to work at Seaside Books.

Second, redo the front window. Take nature out. Celebrate mysteries and detective fiction. It could be fun and edgy. Use crime scene tape. Maybe get a manikin and put a Colombo raincoat on him. A tongue-in-cheek reminder that Seaside Books had a sense of humor.

The 'Help Wanted' sign went back in the window.

CHAPTER 11

Alex wasn't convinced. There was plenty to worry about. In fact, she was still scared.

Crazies with automatic rifles threatened her bookstore. There was no way to make sense out of that. Threatening a bookstore with guns in broad daylight, thinking that nobody would stop them? That's like threatening a library, a pharmacy, or maybe a dry cleaners. What? The whole idea was just so unthinkable. But there they were. And the weird thing was that Seaside Books wasn't the first small business they had threatened.

Their arrogance, their righteous hatred, was appalling. They stood there, a big group of angry old white men with guns pointed at them. Hanging around. They called it rallying, defending themselves. Against what? Books?

Their hatred was obvious. The snide way they talked, like they were entitled to threaten folks, claiming they were defending themselves. They called her "that old lesbo" as if being an old lesbian was an insult. They hated her because she was the owner of a small-town bookstore.

Why hate her? Why? They hated her because they thought she was a lesbian?

Those ugly old men probably never even walked into a bookstore. Did they have wives and children at home? They probably claimed to be normal. Did they take the garbage out, feed the cat, see the kids off to school, and then pick up their weapons and go harass bookstore owners?

So the pending question was whether their failed confrontation was humiliating enough for them to leave the bookstore alone. Ben and the staff's answer was yes. Alex's answer was maybe not.

Alex was thinking somebody else was behind it. Somebody was riling them up, telling them who they should hate, and probably supplying the weapons. On their own, even angry, would they have considered holding a rally outside a bookstore?

Then she got to thinking about the lesbo part. Wasn't that precisely the same phrase that the creep used last year? That old lesbo? Who says that? And another question now popped into her thoughts. How did they know who owned the store?

There wasn't a sign in front of the store saying an unmarried middle-aged woman owned this store. Who knew that? The real estate agent and the title company, of course. Who else? Darlene.

She had been part owner herself. Oh, and Tru knew it. Tru didn't like Alex. Did Tru think she was a lesbian? As far as Alex knew, Tru was the only person in Seaside who disliked her.

Of all the musing she had just done, there wasn't much she could share with Ben. He didn't think in that rambling way like she did. He would become impatient with it. But the detective question always was: who didn't like the victim? In Ben's mind, Alex was the victim. Who were her known enemies? Only Tru.

But Ben listened. It made sense to him. "Maybe Tru thinks he stole Darlene from you, right? Maybe he thinks you two were a couple. Guys think that way. They see two women together. Lesbians. It's all about sex with guys."

Alex said, "Uh-huh. He didn't like me from the start. He asked me why I was called Alex. He even said Alex is a guy's name. How come they call you that?

"So I asked him why he was called Tru. Was it a nickname? He told me it was his name. Tru something. I don't remember. He asked me if we would make a lot of money in a bookstore. Kind of a snide question.

"He's good-looking. Darlene fell for him. Apparently, great sex. XShe wanted a child. Everything was fine between them until the baby came. He was a no-show when she delivered, so I was with her at the hospital. She and Tru got into it. Dar was mad at him too. They split up because of his problems. But he probably blames me."

Ben answered, "Well, isn't that interesting? An out-of-work construction guy with money problems has it in for you. You own the bookstore his ex-girlfriend used to own part of."

Alex told Ben about her recent meeting with Darlene. Dar told her that she was seeing him. She was pregnant again. And he didn't think she got a fair share for her half of the business.

Ben perked up when he heard that. He thought for a moment. He didn't remember seeing Tru at the rally. But that didn't mean anything. He could have had a part in it.

Ben asked her, "What do you know about him?"

"Not much. Not even his last name. He talks a lot about work but is unemployed most of the time. Her contractor didn't think much of him. Not reliable. He has an ex and kids and isn't paying child support. That's about it."

Ben said, "I wonder if he knows those militia guys? I'm also thinking maybe the cops should know this. Maybe he's connected, or at least gave them useful information."

Alex agreed, "It is interesting, and he does have an ax to grind."

The next morning Ben moseyed over to Starbucks, and he noticed that Tru was there in his usual spot. They made eye contact, so Ben went over and sat with him. He said good morning pleasantly and asked, "You look familiar, but I can't place you. My name's Ben."

Ben was dressed in his bookstore clothes. Slacks, a dress shirt, a tie, a button sweater, and wire-rimmed glasses. He looked like an old professor turned bookstore clerk. Totally uninteresting to somebody like Tru.

"Hi, Ben, I'm Tru. I'm a regular here. I come in most mornings. Maybe that's it."

"Oh sure, that's gotta be it. I'm in here, too, just not always at the same time. I work at the bookstore."

Tru continued, "No kidding. That was something the other morning, right?"

"Sure was. Scary. Well, I gotta run. Nice meeting you, Tru."

He nodded. Ben left in a hurry, got into his car, and drove it onto the street in front of Starbucks, parked and waited. Soon Tru came out too, driving a white Ford pickup. Ben followed him at a safe distance. Maybe he was going to work. He was.

Ben jotted down the address and Tru's license plate number and then went home. He'd have some info when he stopped in to see the Seaside police later that day.

Then Ben went to work. Alex and Rishi were opening the store. Alex was counting the cash register drawers, and Rishi was opening mail. Then they would walk the shelves and straighten things up. They'd start removing the nature window. First they needed to pull some books for display. Serena was coming in later with props.

Ben looked at the website to check on updates they might need, and then he'd look at Yelp. He made some notes for Serena. He'd check the bathroom, the break room, and Receiving to ensure all was well. Sometimes stray books landed in the bathroom. A definite no-no. Also in the break room.

Ben was thinking about loading up the fridge with homemade sandwiches for the crew and stocking it with stuff that could be eaten quickly. Maybe sometimes they would prefer to eat in. The running meal tabs were high. Alex paid them without comment. There was also room for a Keurig. They could stock the K-cups, coffee mugs, bottled water, and fixings. See how it worked.

A woman came in and asked about the job. Alex smiled and gave her an application to fill out. Bring it back, and they could talk.

Ben called the Seaside police and made an appointment. The detective would see him in an hour. Ben was excited. This would be his first time in a station for a while. It would be fun to see it.

He left a little later, drove by Tru's job site, and spotted his pickup. Then Ben headed to the station.

The same guy he talked to at the bookstore met him at the front desk. A counter blocked the desk, along with files, phones, and gear. A wall with a window behind him. The chief's office. A long hall with benches lining it. They entered a small office. It looked and felt familiar. Ben was definitely at ease.

Ben told him about Alex and Tru. The cop listened with interest. He was nodding and writing. He perked up when Ben gave him Tru's truck license plate number and worksite address.

"Were you a cop? You act like a cop."

Ben grinned. Gave him a brief rundown. Told him to keep it to himself. He understood. Thought for a minute and then asked, "You want a job?"

Ben laughed. "I wish, but no."

The guy said he'd run the info by the chief. Check Tru's record. Decide what to do next.

The cops checked Tru's DMV records and discovered his name was Arthur Trueblood. They checked Trueblood's police records. Quite interesting. He owed thousands in child support. He had unpaid parking tickets. He once had a suspended license for a DUI and spent a couple of nights in jail for being drunk and disorderly. He was in bar brawls. The neighbors filed noise complaints against him. He was arrested for carrying without proper documents.

The chief decided they should talk to him. He also wondered whether the guys charged with minor violations in the bookstore deal knew him and might be willing to talk about him.

The cops tracked Tru down at Starbucks. He hadn't been at the address that the DMV had for him. When they walked through the door, Tru became suspicious right away. They asked him to step outside. He at first resisted, then thought better of it.

When he heard what they wanted to talk about, he exploded. He had nothing to do with that bookstore deal. They told him they were following up on loose ends, trying to understand what happened. They'd like him to come down to the station. There were a few other things that needed attention as well.

Tru barked, "The station? I gotta go to work. I can't go down there now."

The cop said, "It shouldn't take long. We just have a few questions."

He asked, "Am I going to need a lawyer?"

The cops perked up. "A lawyer? I don't know. Do you? As I said, we're just gathering information. Maybe we talk, and then you decide."

Tru agreed. He followed them. When he got to the parking lot, he called his boss to tell him he'd be a little late. Inside one of the small rooms down the hall, the two cops set up the recorder before starting their conversation with Tru. He was wide-eyed.

"You're gonna record me? What's that all about?"

"We always make recordings. We are going to be interviewing most of the participants. So we gotta make a record."

Tru whined, "I already told you I wasn't there."

The first cop said, "We understand that. But you know the store owner personally. Also, you know her ex-partner. You might have some personal insights that we aren't aware of."

"Well, aren't you guys making a big deal outta

nothing? I mean, jeez, nothing happened."

"We think it was a big deal. It's not the first time it has happened in Seaside. The mayor and the city council are concerned. We'd like to know who's holding these riots and why. Our city's good name and reputation are at stake. Jobs and tourist business are at stake. People are suffering and worried. So we will do our best to get to the bottom of it."

"And I'm supposed to know something about this? I'm laughing my ass off here. I can't help you, okay?" Tru's nervous voice gave him away.

The first cop had the recording apparatus ready to go. He stated the date, the case, and who was in the room. Tru settled into his chair and tried to look bored. They reviewed the identification questions and established that Tru wasn't at the bookstore during the incident.

Then they asked him to explain his relationship with the store owner. "Okay. Her name is Alex, a boy's name. She's Darlene's partner. That's what Darlene said. They were partners. A couple of old lesbo partners come up here from California with pockets full of money to buy a bookstore! A bookstore!"

He explained how he met Darlene in Starbucks.

"Cute, hot for a lesbo. You know? She wanted a sperm donor."

The cop asked, "She told you that before you had sex with her."

"Nah, she just said she'd have sex with me. I didn't know anything much about her when we first started, you know. She just took me up to her loft above the bookstore. Cool place. We got it on. She liked it. I did too. We met regularly. That's when she told me about the bookstore. I thought she was renting the place.

"Anyhow, then she told me she was pregnant. I got scared. I already got a family and an ex-wife. That's when Darlene said don't worry. I consider you the sperm donor.

"That's what she said. It's like, you know, some old lesbo deal. They want a family. They need a man for that. I obliged. Ha ha."

The cops weren't laughing. "So she didn't want child support."

"Well, she did mention it once. But we were fighting by then."

He explained how they had some issues when the kid was born. Her partner was there, Alex, acting like the nervous husband. He was the father, not her. That made him mad. And Darlene got mad too. Alex probably put her up to it.

The second cop was confused. He said, "As I understand it, Alex and Darlene were business partners in the bookstore. Darlene lived by herself over the store. Alex owned a cottage down The Prom a ways."

Tru nodded.

"So they were business partners. Not a lesbian couple. You, Tru, keep using the expression 'those old lesbos'. I've never heard that expression before until this bookstore deal. The maga guy in charge of the rally used the very same expression. I find that a bit odd."

Tru went cold. He started shivering. He tried to talk. Finally he managed. "Come on, that's a common thing to say. Those two were lesbians, no doubt about it. California lesbos."

The first cop said he thought they were finished. They were going to interview the victims next and then the organizers. They wanted to find out what was going on. Probably make some arrests.

Tru said, "What kind of arrests? Nothing happened."

"Well," the cop said, looking at the case file, "several participants were hurt by stray bullets. The guy who shot off his gun was criminally responsible. It wasn't his gun. He was borrowing it. So whoever supplied the weapons would be charged too. And whoever organized the riot has some explaining to do. They were working on charges for that too."

Tru said, "That's all BS. You're BSing me. Trying to work me into something I had nothing to do with. I need a lawyer."

The first cop said, "We're done here. Thank you for your cooperation, Mr. Trueblood."

CHAPTER 12

Tru hurried out of the police station, jumped into his truck, and rushed off to work. It was 10 am. The boss was pissed, but Tru ignored him, put in two solid hours, and then left. It was noon on Friday.

He spent most of those two hours trying not to panic as he worked on his framing job. The cops thought they were so smart. Bang bang. They figured Tru didn't know what they were up to. Tru could figure things out. Bang. They caught him and nailed him with his own smug remarks. Using his nail gun while thinking of being nailed caused him to use too many nails.

Calling Darlene and Alex "old lesbos" was going to fry his bacon. Somebody would cut a deal with the cops and turn Tru in for being the go-between between the militia head and the troops. He had convinced them to hit the bookstore.

He shoulda let it go. He let his anger at Alex get the best of him. He wanted to get even with Darlene. He wanted the store to close, even get smashed up if things got outta hand. That Alex needed to learn a lesson. Too bad the whole thing blew up.

Now Tru was in big trouble, not just with the cops, but with the militia too. They had wanted a different outcome. They wanted the old guys with the guns to be the intimidators. Instead, they looked like clowns. The old guys were scared and pissed off at Tru. What a bust.

Tru figured he had to get out of town immediately. So he headed for the bank, cashed out the checking account, and went to his ex's place. What a dump. Even the garage door didn't work.

He parked in the driveway and pulled up the damned door by hand, bracing it with a long pole. How often had he done that? Once inside, he started loading up his good tools and anything else he could pawn. Then he threw in his sleeping bag, tent, and camping gear. He looked around. He found his duffel.

His ex, Pauline, was there with the kids. "Whatcha doing out in the garage, Tru? You woke up the baby."

"I'm packing a few things. I got a weekend job up in Longview. Good money. I need to take my tools. I should get a good paycheck on Monday or Tuesday. Then you can get the kids what they need.

"I gotta hit the road. You got a twenty on ya? I need some gas to get to Longview and back."

Pauline went to her purse and found the twenty. Better to give it to him than say no. Otherwise, she'd end up with a beating.

"You need some food for the road?" she asked.

"Sure. Could you make me some sandwiches and fill my thermos with coffee? That would be great. I gotta pack a few things."

He went into the bedroom. The filthy carpet underfoot disgusted him. The place was a pigsty. And it smelled worse.

He went to the closet, which was bulging with crap. He packed his best clothes, found clean underwear, went into the bathroom, and grabbed his stuff. He added a towel and a bar of soap.

That'll do. His guns were in the car. He rifled through their papers. Found the title to the truck, his birth certificate, passport, and some other stuff he might need. He looked around.

The lunch was ready. She was filling the thermos. She knew better than to ask him how long he'd be gone. He took off in a hurry. Not even a backward glance.

Next, he went to Darlene's and told her the same story. He picked up a few pawnables from her garage. He grabbed his clothes from her closet to toss in the duffel. He was in a hurry.

"Dar, honey? Can I borrow a couple hundred? I'm flat busted. I need gas to get to Longview and back and a few bucks for a cheap motel. Another guy and me are sharing. You'll get it when I get home. This job pays double time."

"Umm, sure. If I've got it." She went to her purse and counted out two hundred. He watched her. She had a wad left.

"You need a sandwich or something for the road?" Dar asked.

"Oh, god, that'd be great. Whatever you've got. I'm starved."

Dar headed for the kitchen. As soon as she was out of sight, Tru grabbed her wallet and helped himself to a few more twenties.

He called out from the bedroom. "Can I take one of the bed pillows? You know how hard those motel pillows are?"

"Oh, I guess so. Don't forget to bring it home, okay?"

"No problem. I won't forget." He grabbed the pillow and the soft throw she'd left on the chair. He might need that too.

He piled everything into his truck and then went in to get his second lunch bag. He gave her a quick hug and said he'd call when he got there. And with that, he took off.

He got a fill-up and bought a cheap six-pack for the road and was off with the weekend getaway traffic heading south. He'd stop at the pawnshop in Cannon Beach and dump the tools. He might get about $500 cash for them.

So he'd have about $1,500 for his getaway. That wasn't much. He'd have to get a job somewhere. He'd like to slip into Mexico eventually, but he'd need more cash. Maybe his luck would change. Start over, meet someone nice. Make a different life.

Pauline breathed a sigh of relief. Maybe he was gone for good this time. She hoped so. She and her mom had cooked up a plan. Mom would come live with her. Then Pauline could get a job. Mom would be in the spare room. She'd take care of the kids. Her social security would go further if she didn't have to pay rent. They'd fix up the house somehow. Everybody would be better off, especially the kids. Her mom would see to that.

Pauline called her. "He's gone, I think, for good this time. He's on the run."

"I'll be right there, hun. Gimme a few days to get out. We'll make a better life together. I promise you."

"Hurry, Mom. I love you."

Pauline decided she'd start with the cleanup right away. For mom. The kids were playing in the living room. The baby napping. She went outside with a hammer and screwdriver from the kitchen junk drawer. She couldn't help but notice that Tru had taken all the garage tools. That's how she knew he was gone for good.

She used her kitchen drawer tools to remove the screen door. The mesh was hanging off of the frame. It didn't close right. It looked awful. The first thing a person saw when they came over. She eventually got it off and put it in the now-empty garage. Then she got a pail of soapy water, washed the front door, and scrubbed the stoop. Wow, what a difference.

The baby woke up, needing a diaper change and something to eat. The kids got PBJ sandwiches. Then she pulled out the big plastic bags. They'd go outside and clean up the front yard. Baby in the pack-and-play on the porch.

Kids each got a bag. Start loading broken toys, bottles and cans, and other junk into the bags. She began pulling up dead bushes and plants. Tidy things up. Like it used to look when she first moved in. It had been her grandparents' house. At one time it was nice. Not now.

About an hour later, the dead lawn was clean, the dead plants gone, and everything swept up. They stood back and looked at it. Her oldest whispered, "Mom, it looks like somebody else lives here."

She answered. "I know. Some new family has moved in. Us!"

They went inside. There was so much to do. One step at a time. She fixed some dinner. The kids ate it on the living room floor because so much junk was on the dining room table. Tomorrow she would fix that.

When everybody was in bed, she decided to tackle her bedroom closet. It was packed, but she had nothing to wear. She had gained weight since all the babies. It hadn't come off.

She'd read the decluttering book. Twice. For inspiration. Pile up all the clothes on the bed. Sort them. Keepers, garbage, donate. More garbage bags were needed. The only clothes that would return to the closet would be clothes that fit, period. No promises about losing weight to fit into something. Be brutally realistic.

She went to work. And found a few clothes she could wear. That pleased her. The rest mostly went to the trash. She hauled the bags to the garage. She now had a cleared-out closet. She got a broom and some rags and cleaned it. Ick. It had been so dirty. She was ashamed. She grabbed the clothes she could wear and tossed them into the washer. Clean clothes in a clean and mostly empty closet.

Shoes next. She had five pairs of shoes that fit her slightly swollen feet. She wiped them off and lined them up in the closet. Holy crap. What a difference.

She slept well that night. Happy, for once. He was gone. The mound of plastic bags in the garage was growing. She'd have to figure out what to do about that later.

Breakfast was always chaotic. Two kids off to school, and two still at home. They could walk to school and eat free lunches. So just get dressed and eat breakfast. It should be easy. It wasn't. But it will be.

Kids finally off, baby fed and dressed, in the pack and play with her four-year-old brother in front of the tv for the morning kid shows.

She was going to tackle the kitchen and dining room. Start with the tabletop. What was all this junk? It was empty cereal boxes, dirty dishes, mail, old magazines, orange peels, glasses, homework assignments, and her lost keys. Most of it went into the trash.

She found four placemats nearly glued to the top of the table, left there by her grandmother to keep the top from getting scratched or dirty. She had tears falling when she saw those filthy placemats. How could she? Her gramma would be so disappointed. She started peeling them off. They were stuck by spilled drinks most likely.

The doorbell rang. It scared her. Nobody ever came to the door. The kids both started crying. What was happening now? She opened the door. It was the lady across the street.

"Hi! I'm Lydia, your neighbor. I hope I'm not intruding. I'm so sorry. Did I scare the kids?" She was carrying a large pink pastry box.

Pauline said, "Oh, no, you didn't. Well, yes, maybe you did." She tried to smile through her tears.

Lydia stepped in. She tried to cover her reaction to the smell of the place. "Oh, I'm so sorry. I didn't mean to startle the kids. I brought over some donuts."

The little boy stopped crying when he heard donuts. He went to his mom and took her hand.

"The kids love donuts," Pauline said.

Lydia continued. "I want to thank you for cleaning up the front of your house. It looks so nice."

Pauline smiled. "I'm turning over a new leaf. My mom's coming to live with us. I want to clean up the house for her. It's awful in here. One step at a time."

Lydia said, "I've come to help you. I thought something like that might be happening. We noticed your bedroom light late last night. And you were carrying out trash bags."

"Oh that. Yes, I cleaned out my closet. It's nearly empty now. You see, my ex was here to get some stuff. I think he's gone for good now. My life will be different, better, I hope. You came over here to help me?"

"Yes. If you could use a hand. I help people get organized. I'll volunteer because we are neighbors. If we work together, maybe we could finish it by the time your mom shows up."

She looked around and thought, who am I kidding?

"This is a huge job."

"Mom, can I have a donut?"

Pauline looked at Lydia, who handed her the box.

"Yes, let's get you one."

He peered inside. "Can I have that one?" He picked up the pink one with the gooey frosting and sprinkles. And went back to the tv. The baby saw him and howled.

"Oh dear. I'll get you something, sweety". She rushed to the kitchen, found a teething biscuit, and handed it to the baby, who grabbed it.

"What are you working on now?" Lydia asked.

Pauline showed her the table. Lydia surveyed it.

"We better start with that. You know, that's a very nice old Mission-style table. It is worth a fortune in good condition. Let's try to clean it up."

They went to work on it. The spray-on cleaning gunk that Pauline used had loosened the dirt. They were able to scrape it off without ruining the finish. Then they washed off the chairs that also had pads on them. Once they got it cleaned up, Lydia asked if she had furniture polish. Pauline rooted around under the kitchen sink. Came up with some. By the time they were finished, it looked amazing.

"Wow!"

By then, Lydia had seen the kitchen. She told her how she dealt with that kind of job. Just like Pauline was doing. Start with getting rid of the trash, then keep just what you need and toss the rest.

The kids needed attention, so Lydia volunteered to get started on the cupboards while Pauline tended them.

"Be my guest."

The kids needed some play time, lunch, and then naps. By the time Pauline got back, Lydia had unloaded the cupboards, laid out a set of dishes, silverware, and pots and pans that were usable, and had tossed the rest into garbage bags.

Pauline was so surprised. There were gram's dishes, a whole set of silver, and pots and pans. Kid plastic dishes. Glasses, mugs. Three huge bags of garbage.

"No. I don't need to see inside them."

Lydia had cleared off the counters, scrubbed the tile, and stacked up the food that was still good. She had tossed the buggy flour, the moldy crackers, and other stale stuff.

"There isn't much food, huh?"

Pauline and Lydia had talked while they worked, so Lydia had an idea of just what Pauline had been going through. Deadbeat dad, a user, cheating womanizer. She probably qualified for welfare and definitely food stamps. Pauline said she was on welfare but she hadn't updated it recently. They would check into it.

Lydia had snooped into the matching buffet in the dining room and had found another set of placemats. They looked so pretty. Pauline promised not to bury them this time. She vowed to keep the table clear. Pauline heated some water and made a pot of tea. She and Lydia had tea and a donut.

The little kids woke up when the big kids got home from school. So much had changed. The kitchen was getting organized. They smelled donuts. She set them all up with donuts and drinks. More tv and toys came out. They were happy kids.

Pauline and Lydia scrubbed up the cupboards and wiped down the doors. Another huge dirty job. The horrid house smell was lessening.

Then Lydia mentioned the living room rug. It was probably filthy. She had seen rugs for sale at Big Lots. She could probably get one for fifty bucks.

Pauline told her she was broke, but she wanted to get to the ATM before Tru did. He had cleaned out their checking account, but he had one more check coming in. She'd like to snag it before he got it. She needed to run down to the bank and try to withdraw the cash.

Lydia said, "Go now. I'll watch the kids." The kids nodded. Okay with them.

Pauline was back soon. Grinning. She had six hundred and seventy-two dollars. Maybe Tru would forget about that last check. That meant gas for the car and some groceries. She could pay the electric bill. She wouldn't pay Tru's phone bill or his credit card. That would help. She'd get half a tank of gas. She never drove far.

She told Lydia she might hold a garage sale. She was thinking of selling Gram's linens. And some books.

Pauline told her to take the books to Seaside Books. They would buy them from her.

Hmm. Pauline had heard about the bookstore. Tru was always talking about it. Something about cheating a friend. She didn't quite understand the story.

They talked about the living room again. Pauline wanted to get rid of the couch because it smelled awful. And the recliner was broken. She could buy a couch from Goodwill for fifty bucks. Maybe they had a cheaper rug, too. They could pull up the rug and clean the floor. That would make a huge difference. Make the kids eat in the kitchen from now on. Easier to wipe up the spills.

Lydia agreed. The floors got dirty quickly. So much of the dirt didn't come up when you vacuumed. The rugs were filthy. Not suitable for kids.

Pauline wanted to say, 'I don't vacuum,' but she didn't.

Lydia was done for the day. Pauline was so grateful that she cried again when Lydia left. No neighbor had ever treated her so well.

Saturday dawned. Another dreary day. Pauline got up early. The kids would be home all day. So it would be harder to get much done. She would talk to them. Explain that Gram was coming to live with them, so the house needed to be clean for a change.

The kids said, "We will try to be good today and tomorrow."

It was essential to get ready for Gram. What could they do to help?

"Go pick up your toys."

Groan. Could they do something else?

"Yes. Go pick up the backyard, just like the front. Okay?"

Then, could they watch tv and eat the rest of the donuts?

"Yes, if you do a good job."

They ran outside. The baby cried. She plopped the baby in the pack-an-play with some toys and a bottle of milk. That settled her.

So Pauline worked in the living room so she could keep an eye on the little one. She took the pictures off the walls. Oh yuck. Such dirty walls.

She also removed the hated knickknacks. She set them on the kitchen counter. Maybe garage sale items? Lydia would know.

She pushed the furniture off the rug and tried to roll it up. It was stuck to the floor, like the placemats. She found a scrapper and scraped the rug up. What a tremendous job. And so smelly. Finally, it came loose.

She dragged it into the garage. Ooof. The smell. Back to the living room. She got a pail of hot sudsy water and a scrub brush and started scrubbing the floors on her hands and knees. What a long, slow job. But what a difference. She had to keep getting clean pails of water.

The doorbell rang again. Lydia? She hoped so. But come on. She was volunteering to clean another person's house. On the weekend? That is too much to ask. But it was Lydia and her husband. He had volunteered to help too. What the hell. A good cause.

Lydia introduced him. Stan. Stan said he would use his truck to take the trash down to the dump. Really?

Yes, he would. And any old furniture. A friend had a truck. They'd haul it off. Couch? Recliner? They'd take them. Anything else?

Both mattresses needed replacing. And the kids' mattresses too for that matter. But what would they sleep on? Stan said if she bought new mattresses, the store would haul off the old ones. That's the best way to get rid of old mattresses. One at a time. When she had the money. Okay.

The dresser in the spare room was unloaded. The linens, bed sheets, and pillowcases could be looked at later. The guys would take the dresser too.

Lydia helped her finish cleaning the living room floor. The floor was okay. It could use a refinishing, but Pauline couldn't afford that. They just rinsed it well and left it to dry. The house smelled so much better.

The room had built-in bookshelves along one wall. That's where the books were. There were way more books than Pauline realized. Lydia called the bookstore. A guy named Rishi would come over later in the afternoon and look at them.

They had been behind glass for years, so they weren't too dirty. Pauline was afraid they would smell. Rishi could decide.

There were pretty teapots in there too, being used as bookends. They pulled them out. They were heavy. Pauline looked inside. They were filled with pocket change. Grandpa probably did that. They dumped it out on the dining room table. Piles of coins. They started to stack them up. Four teapots' worth of coins.

Lydia said, "Stop. I need to look something up. Where's my phone? Okay. Here it is. I remember this from Storage Wars. Quarters from 1964 or earlier are worth three dollars each."

"What?" Pauline was stunned.

"Yup, no kidding. And dimes before 1945 are worth six bucks."

Pauline asked, "So, we gotta look at all the dates?"

Lydia said, "You might have enough to buy your mom a new mattress. Get your older son in here. Maybe he'll do it."

He came in. Yes, he'd do it if it was for Gram. They set him up. A jar for old dimes and quarters. They needed to get some coin wrappers for the rest of it. For the bank.

They washed up the knickknacks. They looked better now. Lydia called an antique dealer. He'd come right over.

The living room walls were filthy. The men said the room needed painting. Maybe Stan and his friend could do it. They'd work on it today but not tomorrow. Sunday was football day. Okay. Say creamy white paint. Ceilings too? Duh.

Stan and two other guys came in after lunch with paint, drop cloths, ladders, and painter's tape. They prepared the ceiling and walls. Unscrewed the overhead light fixture and the old-fashioned sconces beside the built-ins. Pauline never used them. They just needed new bulbs.

Pauline sighed. She was such a lame homeowner.

Lydia said, "Don't beat yourself up. You've had four children and a worthless husband. Things will get better. We are going to help you."

Pauline was still so amazed. Yes, Lydia was

going to be her friend. Lydia reminded her of one crucial fact. If she kept her house in good shape, the whole street benefitted. They were all grateful that she was finally cleaning up this house. It could be the nicest house on the street. It was a craftsman cottage from the 1920s. It just needed some tender loving care.

By nightfall the painting was done. It looked beautiful. The guys also cleaned up the mahogany built-ins. They had never been repainted. They just needed furniture polish.

Rishi had come by. He worked around the painters. He pulled out all the books. They went through them together. Lydia insisted. Rishi was patient. He explained that the store would pay wholesale for the books because they needed to make a profit. He'd give her a better price than she would get at a garage sale. She knew that.

Lydia was working with Rishi to make sure there wasn't something really special that they should negotiate. He agreed but was glad that most folks he dealt with weren't quite so interested.

He ended up buying all of her books. There were one hundred and twenty books. He paid her three hundred and fifty dollars for them. Garage sale folks are only willing to pay twenty-five cents each per book. Pauline was happy. Lydia was satisfied that she hadn't been ripped off.

The bookstore had customers for these books. Folks who wanted to read the old books. The out-of-print books from another age. These books. He could picture them at the cash register. They would sell for eight or ten bucks each.

The antique dealer looked over the knickknacks. He would pay her two hundred even for them, including the teapots. He offered her eight hundred for the dining room table and two hundred for the kitchen dinette. Lydia said they weren't for sale. He upped his bid to twelve hundred. That would be fourteen hundred altogether. Pauline wanted to sell them.

Lydia asked if they could think about it. He said yes, he wrote the amount on his card and handed it to her. Just call. He'd make the deal. He left with the knickknacks.

They had seventy-five dollars in quarters and a handful of dimes. The rest of the coins were worth about eighty bucks once they got them rolled.

Stan said the paint job was a gift. They'd do the rest of the house too, if they could do it on their schedule. The bedrooms would be easy. The kitchen would be the hardest.

The little kids were mystified. Their whole dirty house was changing so quickly. And these fun people were helping. They played with the kids and brought them presents. Ice cream and cupcakes.

They helped the kids with the backyard so they could include that trash with the big dump run. They found lots of junk back there. More work was needed before the kids could safely play in the back.

They all cleared out at once. The kids couldn't watch tv yet, but Stan would hook it back up for them tomorrow before the game started.

Pauline couldn't believe it. What a day. She had a potful of money. She could buy her mom a mattress, maybe both of them. There were mattress sales going on all the time.

Lydia was knowledgeable about lots of money matters. She told Pauline not to sell the table. Save it for a dire emergency. It was worth way more than the dealer was offering.

She took Pauline and the two little kids to the welfare office and they updated her allotment. She would get four hundred per month, plus more food stamps. Check back if and when she was able to work. Or if her ex started paying child support. That four hundred wasn't nearly enough to live on. But at the moment, she had four kids and no income.

The guys were such softies. They wanted this wretched little family to get a break. If a clean, safe house would do it, they were all in. After they finished painting, they did some plumbing. Small leaks went away, and drippy faucets didn't drip any longer. They checked the furnace, changed the filter, and cleaned it up. The electrical was old but still functional. Pauline wasn't straining the system because she didn't have appliances that sucked it up.

The garage sale brought in several hundred more dollars. Stan took the door off the garage. Nothing was stored out there, so now it was a carport. It sat back from the house and would be safer that way. Just drive in.

Then Lydia had her last brainstorm. She called Habitat for Humanity. Did they still paint houses for poor people? Yes, they did. They would paint the outside of Pauline's house. She could choose the colors. And yes, they had a warehouse filled with furniture. She could shop there.

CHAPTER 13

Pauline had no idea that her new lease on life came about directly from the locally famous bookstore incident. She suspected that Tru, all of a sudden, desperately needed to leave town. She didn't know why. Her main worry had been how to feed the kids, how to pay the utility bills, and how to clothe them properly for school. She had four kids and no means of support. Even though they were no longer married, Tru had shown up often enough to cause them unnecessary grief. He didn't give a damn about his abandoned family. It was an act. When he took her to bed, she felt like a prostitute. She was doing it for the kids. They all breathed easier when he was out of sight.

Now he was gone, maybe for good. Maybe prison. Thank you, Jesus. Please stay away. Pauline's mom had been waiting for him to clear out so she could move in with her loving daughter and needy little kids. A better life was just around the corner for all of them.

Tru told her that he had rented a room somewhere. She didn't know where. If there was a family emergency, she might be able to reach him by phone, but not by address. She also knew he had a girlfriend. She didn't know that the girlfriend had a child with him. Nor did she know that the girlfriend had once been part owner of that very same bookstore.

Pauline was hopeful about her life for the first time in many years. Everybody, especially her neighbors, had thought that the Trueblood fatherless family would grow up to become hoodlums. Once they got to know her and the cute little kids, they realized that she was just a resident who fell under the spell of a serial womanizer. And that given a decent chance, her kids would grow up to be good citizens with appropriate values. The neighbors helped her because they knew her success would be theirs as well.

When Stan and his buddies finished painting the inside of the house and Habitat for Humanity did the outside, the neighbors were astounded. The cottage looked spectacular. Stan, Lydia, and Pauline drove down to the Habitat furniture warehouse and loaded up. She needed so much. Clean mattresses, rugs that could be discarded when they started to smell, living room furniture, dressers, and things to make Pauline's mom feel welcome. A home transformation of epic proportions.

So everybody anxiously awaited the arrival of Pauline's mom and her social security check of fourteen hundred a month. That check, plus Pauline's small welfare check and food stamps, might save them all. The sweet kids had a chance to grow up well enough so that the neighbors' cars wouldn't get broken into, their homes burglarized, or their neighborhood visited by drug dealers and pimps. Was it worth it to help them now? You bet it was.

Darlene, too, got the vague sense that Tru was in some sort of real trouble this time. His usual arrogance was missing. He was in hyper-overdrive to get on the road. She recognized it as pure fear rather than a strong work ethic. She suspected he was going nowhere near Longview, Washington. She would know exactly where he was at all times.

Tru was no techno wizard. He had an iPhone. He used it for phone calls, texting, and sometimes for sexting. He could take photos, but he wasn't interested in showing off how cute his kids were. Nobody would want to make a Shutterfly book out of Tru's dick pixs. Eeeeuuu. There were lots of apps on his phone. He might occasionally play a game of solitaire, or he might make a video call. But for the most part, Tru didn't know or care about all those random apps on his phone. He didn't use email. He couldn't check his bank balance. He had no Venmo or any other helpful app a person might want to use.

So Dar broke into his phone one day. She didn't

need a password. She simply added the app Find My Friends and set it up to let her follow him. She didn't stalk him, but whenever she wanted to know where he was, she was one click away.

Half an hour after he left, she knew he had lied to her. His dot was heading south, not north. She was in her bedroom. Her brand new comfy throw was gone. She laughed. He stole a pillow, her fifteen dollar throw that she had bought at the Grocery Outlet several days ago, and the wad of twenties in her purse was even thinner than it was twenty minutes earlier. He was a sniveling thief and a womanizer, and maybe more.

She didn't know why Tru was in such an all-fired rush to leave town. If she had known that Tru had instigated the bookstore incident, she might have killed him herself. What she did know was that Tru held a grudge against Alex. He had worked up some theory that she had gotten screwed on her buyout deal. In truth, Dar was pleased with the deal and happy to be out of the book business. She hadn't been able to convince her rather hard-headed bed partner that she got a good deal. He should stay in his lane, which was having sex. He was obviously not good at business. Or even construction work, as far as that goes. He was a pretty-boy womanizer. Stick with what you know.

The bottom line was that if the cops ever came to Darlene's door wanting to know where Tru was, she could pinpoint him. A girl never knew when that info might come in handy.

Tru was now somewhere south of Florence, Oregon, in that foggy belt of coastal isolation. The state's southern end was pretty, but the weather was undesirable. He was parked in a desolate KOA. One of a very few intrepid campers. It was so cold and windy that Tru decided there was no way in hell he could crawl into his little tent. So he was stuck trying to get comfortable in the passenger seat of his truck. He had tried the back seat first. No go. The pillow helped, but the throw was useless. He had to get out and find his smelly sleeping bag. While out there, he peed beside his truck. He would not walk over to the John to take a leak. God, he'd have to replace that bag tomorrow. It gagged him. Camping was highly overrated. Maybe it would be better in California. Everything was better in California.

He reached around for his second lunch. He had eaten Pauline's while driving. Peanut butter sandwiches. Jeez. But the coffee was good. No cookies. He hoped Darlene's would be better. What? Cheese and mayo. Christ, woman. Men need real food. A stinkin' cheese sandwich? He pacified himself by thinking of a Denny's grand slam breakfast in the morning and purchasing a Sherpa blanket for tomorrow night. His favorite dream was a woman with her own place, a decent shower, and sex. It was going to be a long, lonely night.

He began to wonder whether he had overreacted. He was more worried about the militia than the cops. Those militia guys were bone-breaking mean. Would they come after him? Nope, not to Florence, Oregon. He was safe from them. Would the cops come after him? Why would they?

They had nothing on him because he had done nothing. He might be connected to the incident in some less-than-meaningful way. He hadn't even been at the scene.

Let's see. What had he done?

First, he had convinced the militia that the bookstore was a good target because they hired illegals, and it was run by lesbians who believed that climate change was real. The militia agreed. A horrible store.

Second, yes, for a price, he would meet with the maga-hatters beforehand and hand out the loaded ARs. Make sure everybody knew how to use them. This militia was lame. Some of them were old farts hanging around the senior center. They were filling in the ranks.

Three, he would deliver the cash to the leader of the group. That's it. Nothing important.

Maybe he could go home tomorrow. Give Darlene her stuff back and the two hundred. Tell her he was sorry. Beg forgiveness. Show her he's a man of his word. Crawl in bed with her. Sigh. Maybe he should go right now. Crap. Why didn't he think things through a little better? He hadn't done anything wrong. He could just turn around and go back home. Well, back to Darlene, maybe.

Ben and Alex were having a late dinner at home. Ben had snuck up to the loft around five to start it. Delicious boneless short ribs. They went into the Dutch oven with onions, carrots, celery, a half bottle of Zinfandel because of its fruitiness, some herbs, and some beef broth. Lid on, into a slow oven. Three hours later, love on a plate, with microwaved little potatoes. And the rest of the wine.

Ben wanted to explain to Alex exactly how things had gone with his police talk. They had been interested in what Ben had to say. It confirmed what they had gotten from the men on the scene. Several had pointed a finger at Tru. He handed out the guns. He was buddies with the leader. No, he wasn't there that morning. The cops also wanted to learn about Tru's connection to Alex and Darlene. The 'old lesbos' remark.

They also talked about Darlene and Tru. They were mystifying to Ben. Less so to Alex. Ben didn't know Silicon Valley culture as well as they did. Social relationships among the nerdiest, most awkward, yet arrogant, group are often short, strained, and sometimes icky. Dating apps proliferate. Usually sex hookups were disguised as ways to find your perfect love match. It happened sometimes, just enough to keep everybody doing it.

When Darlene met Tru, it was a new twist on old-fashioned romance. They met at a coffee bar. They flirted for weeks. They both liked what they saw. Eventually, they had mad, passionate sex, and she got pregnant. Definitely not a Silicon Valley scenario.

Something Ben didn't know: Darlene wanted to get pregnant. She had even advertised on dating apps that she was looking for a sperm donor. It backfired. She met a bunch of scary creeps. Their DNA repulsed her. She gave up. And then voila! She did it with Tru. His DNA was yet to be evaluated. He was a cute guy that she liked, sort of.

Something else Ben didn't understand is that the game of love changes when women are independently wealthy. Both Darlene and Alex were just that. Still are. Hanging around women with money only made Ben slightly uncomfortable. He had his own handsome nest egg.

On the other hand, Tru was penniless. He was

out of his league and out of his lane in thinking that Darlene had been cheated financially. She hadn't been. Alex was her best friend. That's why they chose arbitration. They abided by the outcome. Tru was clueless.

At first, Darlene thought Tru's reaction to the agreement was rather endearing. Then she became annoyed. He was butting into her personal financial affairs. She already knew that he was the one trying to take advantage of her. It grew old. Alex was her friend, not her enemy.

As Alex explained all of this to Ben, he began to understand the big picture a little better. Things were complicated.

By Sunday morning at Denny's, Tru was torn. He could text Dar and find out which way the wind was blowing. If she were at all interested, he'd head back. But he wouldn't call Pauline. Something about Pauline said it was really over this time.

As he sat there with one eye on the screen, lamenting that he would miss the football games today, a breaking story appeared on the local news.

Seaside, Oregon: the militia member from the bookstore incident who was hospitalized had died. A subdural hematoma, or brain bleed, had occurred. By the time he showed up at the ER, it was too late.

Police have been investigating the incident. If anybody has any information about it, please contact the Seaside police.

Tru paid his check and left immediately.

Tru's license photo showed up on the screen. He didn't see it. He was getting into his truck and heading south. The waiter looked at the photo and then at the door and the truck leaving the parking lot. She shrugged her shoulders. Nah. Not that cute guy she just waited on. She forgot it.

The cops wanted to talk to Arthur Trueblood. The victim had mentioned that Tru had handed him his gun. He didn't know how to use it. Now he was dead.

The cops got a warrant for Tru's arrest. He wasn't home. He wasn't where he said he would be. Was he running away from something? They wanted to question him about the gun. Was Tru a gun runner?

The cops visited Pauline Trueblood at her residence, a cottage in a well-established local neighborhood. She told them that she had last seen Tru on Friday afternoon. He was heading to Longview to work the weekend. He was supposed to return on Tuesday.

No, he didn't live with her. They had been divorced for over a year.

No, she didn't know his permanent address. Occasionally he spent the night with the family.

Yes, she had four children with him.

No, he hadn't paid any child support.

Then the cops showed up at the bookstore. Ben was in the back. He took them into the break room and offered them coffee. They declined. They were looking for Tru. They remembered him saying that he had a connection to Alex's business partner. They needed her address and phone number.

"Wait here."

Ben took off. He'd get Alex.

Ben introduced Alex to the cops, who were growing impatient.

Yes, she had Darlene's address.

What was her last name?

Sanderson. Darlene Sanderson.

They wanted her phone number too.

Alex rattled it off.

CHAPTER 14

Darlene's Sundays began early. She had a very full schedule these days. Her little one was coming up on fifteen months. She toddled everywhere, making noises, laughing and crying. She woke early, drank from her sippy cup, and fed herself cheerios and banana pieces while sitting in her high chair. Darlene could have a coffee and toast, check her texts, and get grasp of her day while monitoring her child.

Since today was Sunday, she could keep both eyes on her precious little one. Full attention. They would have a whole day together from breakfast to night-night. She looked forward to it. A walk in her stroller with stops for her to run a little. Peekaboo playtime. Baby fun stuff between eating, naps, storytime, and diaper changes. A full day for both of them. Especially since Darlene was about four months gone with her sister. She needed a nap too. Two daughters, two sisters. Darlene's dream come true.

Tomorrow she would be back to her routine work schedule. Mornings until early afternoons for work and then mom time from three in the afternoon until nine the next day. Darlene thought she could stop working when daughter number two arrived. She felt ready to be a full-time mom with help from her downstairs caretakers. Their arrangement was working well. She liked them. They loved her little girl. They helped with the cooking, cleaning, laundry, groceries, and general baby duties.

Darlene figured she'd stay put in Seaside. Cheap living, close to the beach, to schools, diverse community, no Silicon Valley competitive parenting. A husband would be a bonus, but Tru wasn't in the running. He couldn't tell her the names or ages of his other four. He was just as uninterested in these two.

She would try very hard to break her sex addiction to him. He still took her breath away. She had never been with a man like him. But as a father, he was a miserable failure. A total heartbreaker. She might need some therapy to get over him.

They were getting ready for their walk when the doorbell rang. Dar looked out the side window to see who was there. Two cops? Their car was in the driveway. Crap. It must be about Tru.

She opened the door. They identified themselves and asked to come in. Darlene sighed. An interruption would ruin her day. She grabbed up her little one and dropped her into her pack-an-play with toddler cookies and a picture book.

Hoped they would be quick.

They had preliminary questions about her relationship with Tru. They already knew about his ex and the four kids. Now a toddler and another one on the way?

Darlene said, "Yup. It happens. Some guys are irresistible. Literally."

They looked around. Single woman, lovely house, no mention of child support. Odd. Good mom vibe. She was obviously pregnant and adorable. Happy. Until they asked her about Tru.

Had she seen him lately?

"Yes, Friday. He said he was on his way to Longview to get some overtime."

How long had he spent with her on Friday?

No long because he was packing. She sighed. He needed some stuff from the garage and then the bedroom. Then the sandwiches. She figured he'd been with her for an hour or so. Maybe a little longer. He needed to get on the road. The traffic to Washington could be brutal.

Had she heard from him since Friday?

"Nope."

Was that unusual?

"Nope. This wasn't his residence. He didn't live here."

Did she know his permanent address?

"No."

But he was her child's father.

"Yes," she explained. "Well, technically. He was the sperm donor. I'm the custodial parent. He had no financial or social obligation. Is this information important to whatever it is you are working on?"

The cop answered, "No. It was just background information."

Darlene wanted to know why they needed all the personal information. Why did it matter?

The cop explained, "It's about the bookstore incident. We have some questions. Tru might have the answers."

Darlene was becoming anxious. She wanted to cut this conversation off as quickly as she could. But every question seemed to make things worse. She thought for a minute.

Then she said, "Oh. Huh. Tru has a connection to the bookstore incident?"

"Maybe. So he told you he was going to Longview this weekend?"

"Yes, until maybe Tuesday."

"So he said he'd be back on Tuesday?" The cop was writing in his notebook.

"Yes, that's right."

"And you haven't heard a word from him since he left here sometime Friday?"

"No, not a word."

The cops looked at each other. Shrugged their shoulders. The baby cried. Would she get in touch with them if she hears from him?

Darlene asked, "You mean like a text?"

She smiled and wanted to ask: Did they want to see a dick pic if he sent one? But she didn't.

She felt hysteria beginning to kick in. It occurred to her that she didn't want Tru to be in trouble. These guys were up to something. Were they trying to pin something on him that he didn't do? Tru wasn't into politics. Maga rallies. Protests. Good grief, no.

"Yes, let us know immediately if you hear from him. Here's my number."

She saw them out and sighed. They didn't ask her if she knew where he was. So she didn't have to tell them about the dot. She felt a tear start. What the fuck had he done now? He could be a total shit sometimes, but he wasn't a heartless monster. He was in over his head. She hoped that wherever he was headed, he would stay safe.

She took one last look at Tru's dot. He was on the road heading south toward the California border.

With that, she deleted the app. To keep him safe.

Darlene's first call after the cops left was to Alex. She hesitated for a few minutes before she picked up the phone. She was remembering all those old cop shows she watched. The bad guys always called their accomplices as soon as the cops left.

Darlene hadn't done anything wrong, and Alex wasn't her accomplice. She was her ex-business partner, so it made sense that she would make that call.

She did. And she asked Alex to come over so they could talk privately. Alex said sure, she'd be right over. She showed up twenty minutes later. She figured it was about Tru. She was right.

First, Alex looked in on the baby, who was now taking her afternoon nap. So cute. They both admired Darlene's bump, still small. Her second kid. Dar assured her she was fine. This one would be a C-section too. So no hours of labor first. Then she was getting her tubes tied. So she and Tru could enjoy some nights of pleasure. She didn't want any more babies.

"Well earned, my friend. He must be something."

Darlene said, "You have no idea, unbelievable in bed, such a turd in real life."

They hugged it out. They were both finding their own paths in life. No judging.

Darlene asked Alex to tell her what was going

on with him. Why were the cops after him? Alex filled her in on everything she knew. Including the "old lesbos" remark that would probably nail him as a participant.

Darlene was dumbfounded. "Jeez, that's ugly. He sure had that wrong on so many levels. Does he still think we're lesbian lovers? I gotta wonder what he's thinking when we're together."

Alex told her that Ben was working with the cops to figure out just how involved Tru really was. Darlene figured it was all transactional with Tru. He was just so broke he'd sell out his mom for a couple of bucks. It's easier to be uncompromising when you don't need the money. Tru was easily compromised.

She remembered when he thought he had it figured out. He included the kids in the plan. That was when he thought he was going to marry her. Even that plan was bogus. He decided he could get out of paying child support by tearing his kids away from their mom and dumping them on her. He was just too much. Out of control. He'd never figure things out even if he had money.

They had a good laugh. Darlene didn't know his ex but she doubted that the ex would give up her kids to him and some stranger girlfriend without a whimper. Right? This was the delusional thinking of a man who had no money and no options. Above all, no idea at all about the bond between moms and their kids.

Exactly.

Darlene hesitated for a minute, then asked Alex if she had any idea why Tru felt such anger towards her?

Yup. Alex knew. She was the one sitting in the hospital for hours waiting to hear how Darlene was doing. He was the no-show. That pissed him off. Alex thought he was mad at himself. Alex hadn't done anything. He handed her some man-child victory and left the hospital before he even saw his latest child.

Darlene was trying to make sense of it. "So it was because of that incident at the hospital that caused Tru to sic the militia onto the bookstore?"

"That's it," Alex said. "You heard that one of the militia participants has died?"

"Oh my god, no. What happened?"

Alex said, "Here's the way I understand it. During the incident, one of the guys became agitated and shot his AR straight up into the air. A spent bullet fell back down and hit another militia guy in the head. That injury is what killed him."

Alex added, "The militia guy actually killed someone, yes, and several others were also struck by the spent bullets from his gun."

"My god, that's awful. So that's what sent Tru off in such a hurry?"

Alex, "Yes, probably. Tru didn't kill the guy, but he handed out the ARs to the militia guys. The injured guy claimed he didn't know how to use the gun."

"Oh jeez. The militia doesn't know how to use their weapons?" Darlene pondered it. The whole thing was so incredibly stupid.

"So Alex, how do we really feel about this whole sorry episode?"

Alex laughed. "Do you mean our move to Seaside, or the incident?"

Darlene began to cry serious tears. "What have we done? Why is all this happening to us?"

They were sitting together on the couch. Alex reached over and took her friend's hand. "Hey, Dar. No dark thoughts. It's all going to work out just fine. Try not to worry."

She nodded.

Alex stood. "I'm gonna make us a cup of tea. Why don't you lie down for a little while?"

Dar nodded again. "I need to get up for a minute first."

She tried to stand and felt something. A stabbing pain. A sense of alarm ran through her. Now even more pain. Like a labor contraction. "Oh no! Alex, help me!"

Alex looked at her and felt it too. "What's wrong, Dar. You look so strange?"

"Alex, call the ambulance. I think..."

She looked down. There was blood seeping through her clothes. She screamed.

Alex called 911. And heard the siren almost immediately. She ran for the door and opened it. She stood outside waving at the EMT guys who were unloading bags and a gurney.

And then they were there in the house. She pointed. They examined Dar quickly, asked a few questions, lifted her to the gurney, and told Alex that they were headed to the hospital ER. And left with her.

By then the caretakers were there too, trying to make sense of what was happening. Alex told them she thought Dar had just lost the baby. They cried out. Then the toddler woke up, and she started screaming for her mommy.

The caretaker ran to her room. Alex told the man she was going to the hospital. He understood. They would take care of the baby.

Alex pulled out her phone and got their information, saying she'd call as soon as she knew anything. He said okay.

She ran to her car. The hospital was close by.

She found the ER and emergency parking. She grabbed her bag and ran in. The nurses pointed to the bed but said to wait outside. There was a chair. She sat and called Ben and told him what was going on. She had no information on Dar yet. She'd let him know.

She found a Kleenex and realized she was crying. Couldn't stop. She didn't know how long she sat there. Finally an ER doctor poked her head out.

"Are you Dar's friend?"

She said yes.

"Dar's going to be okay. You can come in for a minute."

Alex stood on shaky knees and walked the few steps to Dar's bed. She looked pale and scared lying there. But she was awake.

Her clothes had been cut off. She was wearing a cotton gown and was covered by a hospital blanket. Her things were sitting in a basket under the bed. Her phone was on the little table.

"Dar. I'm so sorry."

Dar nodded. Tears started streaming down her cheeks. She was making no sound, but silent sobs were wracking her body.

Alex thought: how could this be happening to her sweet friend? Alex noticed several IV drips going into her and a heart monitor displaying her vital signs. She heard a nurse behind her bustling around. She checked every apparatus and then asked Dar how she felt.

Dar nodded okay.

The nurse said she would bring them each something to drink. And then she left. The panel of wires and probes blinked and made weird noises. The readouts flashed information steadily, numbers changing, telling Alex some unfathomable story about Darlene. Nobody else was in the room to watch it.

Alex sat there in the ER room, fingers clutching the chair, she was feeling sick. Alex was stunned. They had been just sitting on the couch chatting. Then boom, Dar was in desperate trouble. Just like that. Was it all the drama over the incident that caused it?

Maybe hearing about Tru and how much trouble he was in was just too much for her. Alex knew that they had some sort of weird bond. It was more than just great sex. She could tell. She knew Dar fairly well. She was usually such a cool cucumber. But no more. She was way more emotional than she had ever been before. Alex guessed that real life was kicking them around more these days. She felt it.

Losing her precious baby was just so cruel. Alex knew that women miscarry all the time. Especially older women. Maybe it was just a coincidence. But what a cruel one.

The nurse came in with two glasses of apple juice. That tasted so good. Even Alex perked up a little. She needed it. Dar was looking a little better. She was relaxing. What an ordeal. It wasn't quite over for her. She needed a procedure. She'd be in the hospital for a couple of days. Crap. Even more bad news.

Eventually, they were ready to move her into a regular hospital room. She'd be doing some tests, and then they'd give her something to help her sleep.

Alex told her she'd go back to her house and tell her housekeepers what was going on.

Dar nodded and whispered a thank you.

When Alex returned to the bookstore, it was close to closing time. Everybody was there. They had all heard the bad news. And they were all sorry. They could tell how upset Alex was the minute she walked through the door.

Ben ran over and held her. She started crying again. The whole day had just been way too difficult. She looked around at everyone, smiled through her tears, thanked them, and pointed to the stairs. Ben followed her.

CHAPTER 15

As Ben and Alex climbed the narrow stairs heading to the loft, once again the Patel kids were left in charge of the store. They just smiled and continued their work.

Serena was creating a drawing of her next idea for the window display. She decided that from now on, unless she was told otherwise, all window displays would be overtly non-political. Simple on the surface, with perhaps covert suggestions that would make liberals happy, while conservatives would miss the point altogether.

The theme was Let a Thousand Flowers Grow. She knew that phrase harked back to the 1960s when the flower children imagined a world where intermarriage was accepted, as were many other non-traditional living arrangements. Flower Power. Today it could be simply about the beauty of flowers.

Current gardens focused on drought-tolerant plants and zero use of pesticides and herbicides, period. Unfortunately, the store had a spotty collection of gardening books. Typically, the older books still incorporated dated ideas and practices. So the store had a dilemma. Move the stock, but stay true to current climate reforms. Nothing was ever simple.

Then she reworked her website updates to reflect the store's social conscience. As far as Serena was concerned, bookstores could be the conscience of the community.

Wedding season was beginning. She had two bookings already. Both were older couples. She hoped that the third one might be Alex and Ben.

Several school groups had requested party dates. Serena and Ellie remained undecided about them. Kids tended to be somewhat unruly. Middle School kids weren't interested in books, so why bother? They were hoping Alex would agree and say no to these requests.

Serena had a more significant personal problem that she couldn't talk to any family member about. It bothered her a great deal, sometimes nearly overwhelming her. She was "seeing" someone. Her first serious romance. She was twenty-three, and according to the family, it was time to find her a husband. An arranged marriage would happen soon unless she met someone on her own, preferably an Indian man.

She had met someone. However, her choice wouldn't sit well with her family or his either. She had been with Jamar for over six months now. She met him at an event. He managed the entertainment at a large corporate party, and she was helping the caterers. They were shy at first but attracted to each other. They flirted during the event and went out together afterwards. He was black and she was Indian. Unusual, of course. Awkward and exotic. Yes. But they were both seeing the stars line up for them.

A friend who worked nights offered his apartment to them for meetups. They were eager, excited, yet profoundly grateful. This would be like a commitment of sorts. She was giving herself to him. He was taking her, and he fully understood what that meant for both rather conservative families. They couldn't wait to be together, no fumbling around in cars or on the beach at night in the dark. Such a dangerous thing to do. They could undress and have sex without worry. That alone made it easier to fall madly in love, which had happened.

They yearned for their nights together while trying to forget them during the day. It was becoming increasingly more difficult to practice safe sex when what they wanted to do was just go wild. They even talked about the "what if" as a serious option. If he deliberately got her pregnant, would the families reluctantly agree to let them marry? It was so tempting.

When they were out having coffee, among others, they could see things more clearly. They were two American adults. They could support themselves. They could find a nice apartment and begin a life together. They could have a bookstore wedding or simply go down to the courthouse. The family must let them live their lives. And choose their own partner.

But even though she saw Ethan and Rishi nearly every day, she couldn't talk to them about her problem. She couldn't trust them to understand and be on her side. No matter what happened, she hoped to keep her job at the bookstore.

Up in their cozy loft with the cats playing at their feet, Alex filled Ben in on what had happened to Darlene. So shocking. All of a sudden she had a miscarriage. It was destined to happen. It just occurred at that moment. Possibly a good thing because Alex was there with her. But still, it was such a heartbreaking thing to go through.

They had been having a good conversation about Tru. Alex had told Dar everything she knew about his part in the bookstore incident, and she got the impression that Dar felt sorry for him. And as a result, she was thinking the same thing. She was wondering if it might be possible to step back a little. Maybe get the police to ease up on their hunt for him.

Ben gave her request some thought. It could be that the incident had become a little overblown. Somebody had died. But that guy had mishandled the rifle, which wasn't Tru's fault. Ben didn't want to be seen as heading up a witch hunt. Maybe Alex and Darlene had a point.

Alex suggested that the bookstore could refuse to press charges against the militia, and specifically against Tru. Ben wasn't sure how much weight that would hold. It would depend on who the victim was. He didn't think the cops had established who the victims were yet. They were trying to please the mayor, who wanted the militia to move on.

The bookstore hadn't suffered. They were scared during the attack but not intimidated. And no physical damage had occurred to them thanks to Ben's quick thinking.

It was the militia that incurred the damage, primarily self-inflicted. They lost credibility over the incident. They suffered a casualty and ended up looking like idiots. Maybe that was enough.

Later that night, after a hurried dinner, Alex could unwind a little. She called the hospital. Darlene was doing well. She and Ben had some wine, played with the bored cats, and went to bed. They were thankful they could walk upstairs and leave the store in competent hands.

As Alex lay there waiting for sleep to come, she remembered Darlene's question. Something about 'this whole sorry episode.' And her reply was wondering whether Darlene was referring to their move to Seaside or was she thinking about the bookstore incident. It was either a large looming question, or a small insignificant one.

Alex thought back to their Silicon Valley days. What was it exactly that convinced them to flee such a good life? The valley's wealth, intelligence, and creativity, along with its diversity and good sense, cocooned them from most of the country's economic hardship and social woes.

The pandemic, of course, affected everybody. But the worst was over when they decided to leave the valley, cash out, and open a bookstore. The bookstore business was something they knew nothing about. What had fueled their overwhelming desire to chuck stable careers and do something they knew nothing about? Maybe it was just burnout plus large bank accounts. Have an adventure, break away. The risk might be worth it.

For Alex, it had been the social part. She was in her forties and had never met a guy that she could tolerate very long. She missed her chance to be a mom and raise a family. Her friends accomplished it somehow. But she didn't. A huge regret there. And she had never had a job she really liked. She was highly skilled, a workaholic, highly paid, of course, but the job was getting to her, as were her so-called friends.

Was that it? Darlene claimed the same problem. Could she have just walked into a Starbucks and found someone? Nope. Silicon Valley Starbucks are all filled with geeks and laptops. It's laughable. There were never any open seats, a remote worker's paradise. She always wondered how Starbucks could stay in business. The workers bought the smallest, plainest coffee and worked for hours. Were they looking for a partner? Nope. They were at work.

Whenever she started thinking of Silicon Valley, her blood pressure soared. The work, ugh. Her little condo and the most annoying HOA board ever. They sucked the joy out of living there. The traffic. Sheesh. Seaside was way better.

Tru was still driving along the coastline, and he was a bit nervous when he crossed into California. But it wasn't a problem. He had freaked out when he saw his photo on tv at the Dennys. He didn't hear the newscast, but something serious must have happened.

He drove through Crescent City. It was cold, and the wind was blowing hard against his truck. No way he was going to stop. Well, maybe for a coffee and to get his bearings. He realized he should have gassed up in Oregon, where gas was cheaper.

He found a McDonald's and a gas station. Now he'd have to pump his own damned gas. God, it was cold. Then he rolled through and got a coffee and some cookies. He had a long drive down the coast before he could slide over to I5. He was wondering if California cops would be looking for him. Maybe it would be better to stay on Highway 1. He wasn't sure. But he was scared.

He was in redwood country. Never been here before. Dark, foreboding trees, gazillions of them, he supposed. It seemed like hours before he got to another town. His plan had been to camp along the way to save money. He was using up precious dollars on gas and still hadn't found warm enough weather to sleep in his little tent. He'd spend another night in the truck passenger seat, struggling with insufficient legroom and that awful-smelling sleeping bag.

Eureka was coming up. Then a thought occurred to him. Wash the damned bag. He drove around and finally found a laundromat. Ta-da. He gathered up his other dirty laundry too, proud of himself for solving the sleeping bag problem without spending much money.

While waiting for his clothes, he tried to think up a plan. Running south just a start. What would he do once he got there? Would the cops still be looking for him? And why? Was what he did with the militia criminal? The militia usually got away with whatever they did. So why were the cops picking on him?

Focus, dammit! What next? Could he get a job and make some money? Start a new life down here? Probably not. Maybe there was some kinda day labor he could get, work his ass off, like the Mexican illegals do, and hope to get paid at the end of the day. Stand out in front of the hardware store yelling: pick me, pick me.

Maybe what he should have done was talk to the cops and clear things up instead of running. Perhaps he made a wrong decision with the militia. He wasn't a criminal. Right?

Should he turn around and go back home? Huh. He really didn't have a home. He'd been toggling between Darlene and Pauline, lying to both of them. Two good women with kids, his kids. And he couldn't take care of any of them. What on earth happened that got him into this much trouble?

He couldn't go back to Pauline. He left her flat broke with four kids in that dump. How could he have done that? They deserved better than him. At least she had a home. It had belonged to her grandmother. He tried to convince her to mortgage it so they could live off the loan money. He had some nonsensical idea about making a killing with the loan money. He was glad now that she said no because his big idea had been a scam.

Then Darlene. Lucky her. She had a pile of money and a house. And a job that paid well that she could do at home. He picked up his phone and called her. She answered after a few rings. He could barely hear her.

"Ya gotta speak up. I can't hear you. Are you sick or something?"

She said, "Tru, is that you?"

He said, "Yeah, it's me. What's wrong? You sound funny."

She told him that she was in the hospital. She lost the baby. She started crying.

"Oh, jeez. I'm sorry. Are you okay?"

She told him she'd be okay in a few days. She wanted to know where he was and when he would be home. The cops were looking for him. He told her he'd be home as soon as he could. Tomorrow or the next day. Home! Her home! At this point any home would do.

He folded his laundry and smelled his sleeping bag. Ahhh. He piled back into his truck and headed north. Maybe it was time to do the right thing.

CHAPTER 16

Early the next morning, Ben hurried off to the cop shop to talk to his buddies. He wasn't sure how they would take the news, but he could try convincing them to see things his way. He decided to go with the 'who's the victim' angle and see how it went.

Ben began without apology, simply saying that for the good of the community, the bookstore would not be pressing charges against the militia because they didn't feel like they had been victimized. There was no physical damage to the store and no loss of business either. The incident seemed to have blown over. They'd like to move on.

Also, Ben felt the same way about Tru. It could have been a misunderstanding. It made them very uneasy to have gone after Tru for a few unkind remarks. And he was the father of Alex's dearest friend's child. Darlene was very upset about the whole thing. So much so that she had a miscarriage a few days ago, a devastating outcome.

The cop said nothing as Ben talked. Ben was

usually a man of few words, like most good cops. But he figured he should act less like a cop and more like a private citizen this time.

"Tell Ms. Sanderson that we are sorry for her loss, sincerely." The cop thought for a moment, shifting his papers, before speaking further.

"Your bookstore not pressing charges is certainly surprising. But to be honest, we tend to agree with you. The whole deal has been strange. We don't think it's much of a case either. If this Trueblood guy hadn't left town like he did, we wouldn't be so eager to see him.

"You got any idea when he'll be home?"

Ben answered, "No, I don't, but he told Darlene he was leaving for a weekend job. He's not supposed to be home for a few more days. So it could be true, and he'll eventually show up, especially since his girlfriend is now in the hospital.

"Do you think this could get back-burnered for a while? Say until you hear from him?"

The cop said, "Yes, I think we can do that. Between you and me, the chief would be happy to see this one buried somewhere."

Ben smiled, "I won't say a word."

Ben and Alex huddled together on the couch as he told her about the conversation. Alex was thinking about what a dear man he was. He listened, he analyzed, and he acted. He didn't minimize things, or act like he was uninterested.

Alex picked up her phone and called Darlene at the hospital. Dar sounded better. Alex told her to get in touch with Tru. Convince him to get home quickly and go straight to the cops. If he did that, he'd be out of trouble.

Darlene said thanks. Whatever Alex had done to make this happen, she was grateful. She wouldn't forget. She'd make the call to Tru.

Things were going well at the bookstore. Customers stopped by before heading to Starbucks or the diner. Just like Alex had envisioned it even before they opened for business. Her customers went off to dinner with something from her store.

Murf popped in one day on her way to visit the pawnbroker. She and Alex ducked into the diner for BLTs and book talk. They hit it off so well. Alex was always learning something from her.

Alex wanted to hear about the ethics behind the resale business. She was buying used books and reselling them. She sometimes felt a pang of uneasiness about buying low and then profiting off of other folks' small treasures. Murf didn't laugh off her concerns. She explained her point of view on the book business using popular tv shows to make her point.

"Buying something cheaply and then reselling it

for a profit is the goal, right?" Alex nodded, biting into her delicious sandwich.

Murf continued. "You've heard of Antiques Roadshow? Viewers have been watching it for years. The folks who bring in an item for appraisal are always asked where they got it and how much they paid for it, right?"

"Uh-huh," the French fries were good too. Alex was beginning to see where Murf was going.

"Viewers especially like to hear about garage sale finds where some hapless homeowner sells a valuable painting for a few bucks. Nobody criticizes the transaction. Not at all. In fact, most folks prowl around garage sales and thrift shops hoping to find that elusive deal too. Just like when you two found those rare books."

That hit home. Alex did feel bad about that. Murf giggled. "Don't. You hit the jackpot that day. We are all jealous."

Then Murf mentioned Storage Wars, another long-running show based on the same idea. If folks don't pay the rent on their storage units, the units are eventually auctioned off. Bidders face off to buy the units and then hope they will find something of value, and make a profit by selling it.

Alex chuckled. "You gotta be kidding. There's a tv show about buying used crap out of storage lockers?"

"You should watch it. It's been on for years."

Alex made a mental note. Watch Storage Wars.

The concept was more straightforward now. She saw where her store fit into the business, so she took it in stride. It was just another form of capitalism.

As Murf explained it, the lure of these shows was two-fold. First, to amaze the viewers by how much can be made selling old stuff, and second, to make the viewers aware of the possible value of things they own, possessions that they take for granted.

Alex listened closely to her friend Murf, whose bookstore in Portland did very well. This was new information to her. She hadn't heard of Storage Wars. Imagine. Not only were these folks making money reselling used goods, but they were tv stars. She did know about Antique Roadshow. At times she did feel bad about clueless garage sale deals.

So Alex's bookstore was part of the group that resold books, hoping to profit from someone who needed to get rid of books. The profit was small. She figured she was in the recycling business, not the business of scamming wealth off of the unlucky. She was buying books that folks donated. Books they no longer wanted. It was only after finding and selling the Latin books at such a massive profit that her social conscience kicked in.

Everybody understands that it's finders, keepers if an unexpected treasure pops up. But Murf added that it was all about finding the right buyer for the treasure, and often that buyer doesn't show up.

Alex thought it was all fascinating. She had created a venue for selling used and new books. Books that needed a new home. She would stop worrying about cheating people.

In the meantime, Tru was on the way back home. He had heard from Darlene. There was a possibility that he wouldn't end up in jail after all. He'd have to say and do the right thing and hope his luck had turned.

It was a long drive, but by afternoon Tru was in Seaside. A weak sun was trying to peek through the prevailing overcast. To Tru, it was the same old Seaside, but just maybe it could be his home again. He did as Darlene suggested and pulled into the parking lot of the Seaside Police Department the minute he got into town.

He looked at himself in the rearview mirror. He looked haggard with a four-day beard and bags under his eyes. His clothes were rumpled. He reached over the seat for his jean jacket and ran a comb through his hair. He found a mint in the glove box. Standing outside the truck, he did a few stretches and pulled himself together. He didn't look all that bad. He might have lost a few pounds, and he was slim to begin with. He could possibly pass for someone who had put in a few days of hard labor.

He tried smiling but couldn't. He remembered Darlene. He needed a serious look for serious times. He was a man in a hurry.

He went into the office. The front desk cop recognized him. Tru politely told him who he was. The cop picked up the phone. A minute later he was in the familiar office facing the same surprised cop.

"I heard you guys want to talk to me. I just rolled into town. What's up?"

"Yes, we have a couple questions for you."

The cop looked through some files on his desk, opened one, and said, "Oh, yes. Did you hear that the guy who was injured that day in front of the bookstore has died?"

Tru stared at the cop. "Jeez, no kidding. I hadn't heard. I've been out of town. That's too bad."

"We heard you sold him the gun."

Tru blinked. "Well, you got that wrong."

He thought for a minute and said, "No, I handed him a gun. There's a difference. I was at a meetup with the militia guys. A couple of old guys were in charge. They had rounded up some local folks and convinced them to be in the militia for a day. They didn't have guns. The old guys had a box of them in their pickup. They both had bad backs."

The cop was looking at Tru with interest. He hadn't heard this before. It sounded dumber than hell but totally authentic. When perps were telling the truth, it often was so mundane that it had to be true. That's what he was hearing. Bad guys with bad backs. The ring of truth.

Tru continued. "So they asked me if I could jump into the back of the truck and hand out the guns. They were just borrowing them, ya know? So I did that. They were just for show. Nobody was supposed to actually fire them. That was made clear. So that's what I did. Opened the box and handed them out the ARs to the old guys.

"The militia leaders had asked me to tell them about the store and this uppity woman running it. They knew about her. So I told them what I knew. I wasn't interested in going with them. They gave me fifty bucks for my information, and I left. That's it."

The cop asked, "Why didn't you tell us this the first time?"

"You didn't ask."

"Okay. That's helpful info. We shoulda heard that earlier. We're putting this case on hold for a while. But if those guys come back, we'll come looking for you."

Tru said nothing.

The cop said, "Look, we're sorry to hear about your girlfriend. Really sorry, man."

A tear sprang up, rolled down Tru's cheek. He knew how heartbroken Darlene was.

"Yeah, thanks. It's tough, ya know?"

The cop was wrapping it up. "Look, you got some responsibilities. You got needy kids. Figure it out. I don't wanna see any non-support paperwork about you crossing my desk. If I do, you'll be in the lock-up fast. Got that?"

"Yes, sir."

Tru was free to go. He got all the way to his truck before breathing a huge sigh of relief. He had essentially told the truth. He knew it sounded real because those creepy militia guys were just a stupid bunch of old farts who imagined themselves to be big shots. That the guy died was a tragedy. But it was stupidity that caused it.

He got in the truck and called Darlene. She was home. Could he come over? Yes.

Back in the store, Alex sat down with Ethan. She had a small stack of applications. Ethan had written up a few notes on them. She wanted his input. She separated them into male and female. She had wanted to hire a guy, possibly middle-aged. Any chance of that?

Ethan looked over the male applicants. Hmm. He pulled one out. A local, semi-retired postal clerk. Ethan said he looked like he belonged in a bookstore. Very quiet. Thin, walked with a limp. White guy. Sort of shy.

Alex was skeptical. "Would he fit in?"

Ethan said, "I think he'd disappear."

Ethan handed her another application. "I like this guy. Logan. He's young, has a great smile, and is out of school. He says he could work evenings. Likes bookstores. I think he's Filipino. He would definitely fit in."

Ethan looked over the female pile. "Oh, this one. A friend of Ellie's. She'd be interested in an internship. She's Ellie's age. She could work with Ellie and learn the ropes. We could give her a monthly stipend.

"And this one, a mom looking for work during school hours. Can't work summers, just school days. But I think she'd be good. The problem is the school year is nearly over."

Alex mulled things over for a few minutes and made some calculations.

"That's an interesting list. I'd like to see all the

guys, the intern, and the woman. I figure we could use her in the fall, through Christmas, at least. Can you call them and schedule interviews? I'll be around most of this week."

"Uh-huh." Ethan was happy. "If we can afford it, I like the idea, especially the part-time guy. He'd be a great addition for weddings. He's got a very friendly look."

"Great, set them up. There's always so much to do around here. Oh, by the way, are you and Ben set to check out that estate sale later this week?"

"Yup."

"We gotta get some new people in here. I just realized that none of you have had any time off since we opened. We need to do something about that. That's the thing about startups: there are no procedures in place for the routine stuff. I probably need to schedule review meetings with each of you. Can you work that into the schedule too? I want to do one-on-ones with all of you."

"Okay, boss. I'll figure it out and give you the schedule. Is there anything else I've forgotten?"

Nope.

Tru just opened the door and walked into Darlene's house. She was alone, lying on the couch. It looked like she had been sleeping. She saw him. Tears started trickling down her cheeks.

"Hey, hon. I just left the cops. They don't need to see me. It's gonna be okay." He sat on the coffee table and took her hands. They were cool and rough. Bandages where drip lines had been.

She looked tired and grief-stricken. He looked around. She was definitely alone. "Where's little Amy?"

"She's downstairs. We haven't told her that I'm home yet. I need a day or two to get back on my feet. I won't be able to pick her up for a while. Doctors orders. I don't know how we'll work that out."

Tru said, "Maybe I can help. About time I got to know her a little better, don't you think?"

She nodded. It hadn't occurred to her that Tru might help out. She would have to think about that.

She asked him what the cops had said. He told her about the visit. How they were rethinking the case. He wasn't in any trouble. Tru didn't mention the cop's warning, but he wouldn't forget it soon.

She was pleased. She noticed how tired and gaunt he looked. He dismissed it. He didn't want her to know exactly where he had been or that he had been seriously considering never returning. Especially now that he was back.

He might fess up one of these days but not now. He wanted to be a better man, but one step at a time. Try this first. Help his girlfriend. Don't duck out. Do the hard things for once. See how it goes.

CHAPTER 17

Alex was trying to remember what exactly it was about bookstores that she liked the best. What came to her was a list of things she disliked about them.

The unreliable bookstore: When the closed sign is still up, even though the store hours painted on the window says it's supposed to be open.

The musty bookstore: The store makes her sneeze from the mold spores in the air.

The dirty bookstore: Grimy stores with filmy windows and books stacked on the floor.

The unfriendly bookstore: the clerks don't say hello or acknowledge her when she has a question.

Snooty bookstores: the customer is beneath their dignity, or they are too busy on the phone to talk to an actual customer.

Unorganized bookstores: the book is there, but the clerk can't find it.

Uncomfortable bookstores: no chairs, no restroom.

Luckily, her store made sure that most of these no-nos were taken care of. Her dedicated and reliable staff saw to things that mattered. Sometimes they just couldn't do everything. So she decided it was time to concentrate on getting them some help and paying more attention to them.

Her first review was with Ethan, her first employee. They talked about what his plans were now that he had finished up community college. He was thinking practically these days. Trying to juggle bookstore hours with training that he thought he'd need in the future.

Eventually, he wanted to own a bookstore. There was a lot to learn, business strategy, for example. He talked to counselors about an accelerated program to get him his bachelor's and master's in business in the next two years. Most of it could be done online through various school programs. A new way of getting degrees tailored for students with firm goals and good grades.

Alex was so impressed. He was working up a timetable to fit things in. He wanted to stay with the bookstore because it gave him a hands-on perspective that would be useful for his career goals.

She would look forward to seeing the schedule and ensuring he had time for his studies. He also received a raise and a two-week vacation. Use it whenever he wanted to.

Next came Serena. She was on a whole different track. She asked if she could speak confidentially with Alex about a personal problem. She wanted to keep her bookstore job, but her life had suddenly become overwhelming, and she was frightened.

"Oh dear, how can I help you, Serena? You are one of my most valued employees."

Serena smiled to herself, thinking about their rather foolhardy plan. They had decided to get her pregnant as soon as possible. They had become obsessed with the project. And, of course, it worked.

She was pregnant and feeling great. They had found an apartment and were renting it. A wonderful little two-bedroom that they adored. They hadn't started living in it yet. They were driving to Warrenton to a Justice of the Peace to get married.

Alex was waiting for the punchline. This all sounded routine to her. What was the problem?

Their bitter families, especially Serena's. That was the problem.

"You see," explained Serena, "my dad will be outraged when he finds out I'm pregnant without being married. That's bad enough. When he finds out I'm married to a black man, he's going to go into a murderous rage. Now that there's no turning back, I'm really scared."

"You're serious, aren't you?"

She nodded, and tears started falling.

Alex was perplexed. There wasn't anything she could do except wish her well and hope that things worked out okay. Alex could be very flexible with her work schedule, especially when her due date got closer. The bookstore had a plan for maternity leave. They would implement it. They would do whatever they could to support her through this rough patch. Perhaps she needed a few days off right now to concentrate on family.

Serena thanked her for that. It definitely would be big help to take a week now. She wanted to talk to her mom and maybe connect with her friends to get some help moving into their place.

Alex agreed. Take the time off. Getting settled into their apartment was important, especially if she was feeling well at the moment.

Serena was grateful. She would leave now and check in regularly.

Good idea. Alex made some notes to remind her about Serena's future needs. And she was relieved to know that she had a list of potential employees waiting in the wings. She needed to get them hired as soon as possible.

Serena left the bookstore in a hurry. There was so much to do. She headed home to talk to her mom while her dad was still at work. She thought maybe if she broke the news to her mom first, Mom could get Dad to come around. They intended to drive to Warrenton tomorrow. The big day.

Her mom must have known something was up. There had been too many nights when Serena came sneaking into the house so late it was nearly morning. They had to talk.

The kitchen table was crowded with the usual clutter. Bottles of hot sauce, a glass full of silverware, a stack of clean bowls, and spices. Her mom set out the teapot and cups for them. Her mom looked old. When did that happen?

Serena told her she was pregnant. Mom gasped. "Oh no, Serena! How could such a thing happen?"

Serena tried to make light of it. "Mom, the usual way. I have a boyfriend. We are very serious about each other. We have been making love for a while now. It happened."

"My dear. Do you have any idea what your father will say?"

"Mom, I'm a grown-up. I'm no longer daddy's little girl. I get to make my own decisions."

Mom countered her, "You know that your dad doesn't believe that. Tell me who it is? Do we know the boy?"

"No, mom, you don't know him. His name is Jamar, and he's African American. Light skinned, like Obama. Dad liked Obama, right?"

Serena's mom was sitting there like she had been struck by lightning. Her hair was standing on end. "How could you do such a thing? Our daughter? Your father will kill him."

"Mom! Don't even say that. I love him. We are going to be married tomorrow. Mom, make dad understand! It's my life. We even have our own apartment. It's close to work. Here's the address."

She went to her room and started packing the rest of her things. She had been removing them little by little. She found her old luggage in the back of the closet. She tossed things into it from her chest of drawers. The rest of her hanging clothes went into a large garbage bag. Shoes and purses into her dirty clothes basket. Bathroom items into a tote bag. A few miscellaneous items went into another tote bag.

She made several trips out to the car. Soon she was ready to go. Mom had calmed down a little. She was crying and moaning softly when Serena came in to say goodbye.

Her mom tried to smile but started sobbing again. Serena began backing out the door. Her mom said, "Wait. I want to give you something. I don't know if I'll get another chance."

Serena stood in the doorway watching her beloved mom. Her heart breaking for what she was doing to her. Mom opened a cupboard door. There were vegetables and soup cans in there. She found a can of tomato soup. Nobody liked tomato soup in her family. That can had been there a long time.

She pulled it out. Sat down and looked at it and then at Serena. "This is my hiding place."

She popped open the top. Inside was a big wad of cash. "I've been saving this for your wedding." She handed it to Serena. "I know you will need it."

"Oh, thank you, mom. You will like Jamar. You will see. And you will be a grandma. It will all work out." She hugged her mom and left. A little glimmer of hope and some money. Maybe enough for some used furniture.

Jamar and Serena drove to Warrenton and were married in a quick civil ceremony, paperwork properly filled out, and unknown witnesses thanked. They stopped at a seafood restaurant on the way back to Seaside. Tonight would be their wedding night, and they would spend it in their new apartment.

Serena was now wearing a narrow gold band, so was Jamar. They kept grinning at each other. Mission accomplished. Husband and wife with child, and their apartment waiting for them. Their new life was just beginning.

Jamar told Serena his family story. Their reaction was more like disappointment than rage. Pats on the back, good wishes, but a certain sorrow, knowing that Jamar had chosen a difficult path.

Their apartment was on the second floor of a two-story building. Reserved parking in the back. Two spaces side by side for them. Serena's car was there. Jamar parked beside her. He carried a small bag of groceries for tomorrow's breakfast. They would have their work cut out for them during the next few days. They needed everything. He told her he'd call a friend with a pickup to make the job a little easier. She was nodding, feeling tired all of a sudden.

At the front landing to their stairway stood a group of people bearing various gifts and boxes.

"Oh," said Serena, "I recognize some people. Friends of mine. Look, yours too. How did they find out that we got married today?"

Then Ellie and Ethan popped out and started waving. They had been sworn to secrecy. So they created a party. A wedding and help-you-move-in party.

Lots of laughing and cheering. They all trooped upstairs. So many people were there, and they were bringing so many things with them. Serena and Ethan were utterly shocked.

Ethan said, "You haven't seen half of it."

A rent-a-van showed up, a rather large one. More friends drove up. The guys started for the van, which was filled with furniture. They explained that it was not new stuff, just odds and ends. Somebody had this, somebody had that, and soon they needed a truck. A quick stop at the Goodwill. You're gonna be surprised. And they were.

They stood at the door as each gift arrived. Ellie had kept track of who gave what. She announced things as they showed up. The crowd acted as decorators, deciding what went where, no there, a little further, now back half a step. Perfect. Like that, with everything. Polishing cloths came out, vacuuming happened, and floors got swept. Windows wiped off.

The parade kept going. A couch came in. Clean, not broken down. Lots of snoozin' still left in it. Brown tweed. Okay. A throw rug in front of it.

New! From the Grocery Outlet. The apartment was fairly new, so there were bare floors. The tile that looks like wood.

A couple of end tables, not matched but in good shape. A coffee table. Small but handy. Next, a kitchen table and four chairs. They needed a little elbow grease. A respectable, clean high chair. Howls of laughter. Already. Cheers!

The women were busy in the kitchen unwrapping a set of Goodwill dishes, pretty, but dated. No matter. Other things for the kitchen. Somebody was washing them up. Pots and pans, cookie sheets, Tupperware, Corning ware, coffee mugs. Gadgets. It all got a wash and polish. Women huddled around the drawers, deciding what went where. So much serious fun.

A recliner showed up. It still worked. It was leather. Out came the leather cleaner. Somebody took charge of spiffing it up. For Jamar. The guys made him sit in it and took photos for Instagram.

Linens, towels, small lamps. A bookcase filled with books from the store, with Alex's best wishes. Baby books. For Serena: mysteries and children's books.

Click click. Glassware, a bar cart, booze, bottles of wine.

Pantry food. A set of knives. A Keurig, with k cups.

And finally, Serena and Jamar had to stand by the door with their eyes closed while the last gift appeared. An awkward fit through the door. Lots of whispering. Running around, up and downstairs. Keeping eyes closed, they led them to the extra bedroom. Then finally they could look. Ta-da. A full nursery. A family graduated their last kid to a real bed. They couldn't wait to pass the baby stuff along to another expecting family.

Serena opened her eyes and cried more tears. It was so pretty. Even more tears from all the other mothers. Hugs and exclaiming, talking all at once.

The neighbors came by to see what the heck was happening. Cheers went up from them too. Soon a few more gifts arrived. A small bistro table and two chairs for their balcony. And the last gift, a well-used but still streetworthy stroller, came in. The folding kind that was easy to get down the stairs.

The pizza showed up, and the cupcakes and soft drinks, also courtesy of the bookstore. People love to give wedding presents but seldom are their friends so in need of everything. It had been a last-minute pleasure to run around town finding used household items for their friends.

Perfect gifts that they knew would be appreciated. A grand party, one of the best wedding receptions ever. Finally, the last story had been told, the last bargain accounted for, and the final donation recorded. It was time to leave. The house had been cleaned and arranged. It was ready for a brand new family.

Serena and Jamar fell into bed, grateful beyond words. They could sleep in and get up knowing they were in a real home. How lucky for them.

The local news got word of this most remarkable wedding reception and knocked on their door the next afternoon. Could they hear the story and maybe take some video? It was such a heartwarming story.

Of course.

Serena showed them in. They had questions, and some were a little too personal as far as Serena was concerned. They ducked them and concentrated on the overwhelming kindness of their friends.

That night the story appeared on the news. With a lovely picture of the bride and groom holding hands and talking about their new baby on the way.

Everybody in Seaside thought it was a remarkable story of young love. All except one household. When Serena's dad saw her on the tv holding hands with that black guy, he went into a rage. He was going to kill the bastard. Serena's mom was frantic. He had been drinking all day, now this. He got his gun out. He was going to go over there and shoot him. That's what he was gonna do. Now.

"No", she said, "give me that gun. You don't mean that."

He pushed her away. She got up and lunged again, he really pushed her hard. She went down, stunned for a minute. This was bad.

She found her phone and called. Serena answered. Mom told her that her dad was on the way over there. Don't let him in. Call the cops quickly. Their lives depended on it. He seemed dead serious. She was right behind him.

Serena's dad found their apartment. He pounded on the door. They told him to go away. The cops were coming. The other neighbors looked at him standing outside their door with a huge handgun and slammed their doors. Lots of 911 calls went out.

He heard the sirens and ran back downstairs. His rage increased. How dare they call the cops. This was a private matter. His honor was at stake. He needed to handle this ugly piece of business one way or the other.

He was standing right below their balcony. He hollered her name.

"Serena! Come out, dammit!" She needed to hear that what she was doing was wrong. She was shaming the family.

The cops showed up and saw the angry man with the gun. They went into emergency mode. It wasn't often that out-of-control drunks started waving guns at their own kids.

Next, the wife drove onto the scene. She pulled up near her raging drunk husband. The cops were on the far side of the street in back of the angry dad, wearing their flak jackets, hiding behind their car doors, and using their mics to get his attention. He suddenly turned. He was still waving his gun. He looked at four cop cars with officers pointing their firearms at him.

"Drop the gun. Hands on your head."

Over the noise, he heard his wife pleading with him.

"Please listen. Please don't do this."

Dad made one last attempt to get his daughter to step out onto the balcony. He just wanted to talk to her. Please come out. The balcony door opened.

He laughed and took aim. Mom screamed, "Nooooo!"

He turned and looked at her.

"Shut up, bitch."

He then aimed at her. She ducked down just as he shot out her driver's side window. Then he turned on the cops, aiming at the chief's car. A single shot rang out and hit him in the heart. He went down.

It was over.

The local news didn't show up in time to catch

the shooting in progress. Only two shots had been fired. They found lots of witnesses who told them the story they saw. The neighbors, the cops, other interested bystanders. None of them could piece together precisely why the dad was so angry.

The police interviewed the shooter's wife. She refused to talk to the news people. Serena didn't either. Her dad was dead, killed by the cops. Her mom was hysterical. And everybody wanted to know why it happened.

The cops would write it off as a domestic problem that got out of control due to alcohol. No other details were ever given why this angry father would become the victim of a police shooting. Those on the scene saw him take aim at the chief. He had already shot once at his wife. It was a righteous take down.

Serena and her husband went away for a couple weeks. Their honeymoon. A hastily arranged trip down the coast. When they got home again, the dust had settled. Serena and her mom talked, the kids all got together and hashed it out. They would not blame Jamar in any way. They all knew about their dead father's temper. In time they would forget about it.

CHAPTER 18

By June the dust had settled. Serena was feeling better and working again. She had warned Jamar months earlier that her dad was a racist, but Jamar was mentally unprepared for what had happened. He and His family were mystified. Jamar had done nothing wrong. Their wonderful son did not deserve to be subjected to that spectacle.

But for Jamar's sake, they tried to find a way to accept Serena despite her father's outrageous behavior. Racism often reared its ugly head, but not to that degree. Not in their family, at any rate. It would be a long healing process, as far as they were concerned, even though the bastard was dead.

Between Jamar and Serena, they tried to brush it aside. They were beginning their new life. They received lots of sympathy from their friends and relatives alike. That helped.

Being married was everything they thought it would be. It was wonderful just to be together. They wanted to forget the awful incident and move on. They had commitments, a child on the way, and good jobs.

Their apartment was adorable. The furniture they received needed a few personal touches. They found artwork, window coverings and throw pillows for color. They would always be grateful for the head start they received from their most thoughtful friends. Think about that. Don't think about the horror of that night.

Serena found out they were having a little girl, so she started buying baby clothes and necessities. It was enjoyable because her mom did it with her. They had made up. Mom swore she didn't feel the way her husband did. She was going to be the best mother-in-law ever.

Serena's mom cried a lot at first. That was difficult for Serena. She was still processing her dad's hatred of a man he had never met. A man his daughter loved. He hadn't been a good dad. He had been dictatorial, a penny pincher, and he never acted like he loved the kids or his wife. They were possessions.

Dad had become more difficult as his kids got older. He beat their mom, which she never mentioned to the kids. He drank too much, and his anger overwhelmed them. They would never understand why he picked up his gun that night. When had a gun ever fixed a problem? He couldn't browbeat Serena, so he would kill her husband? Or himself?

Mom decided to sell the family home with all of its bad memories. There was a sadness about it. If she sold out, she could rent a little apartment close to Serena. Just take what she needed and get rid of the clutter and junk of the past forty years. She hoped she could help Serena when the baby came and be a perfect mother-in-law. Make up for her husband.

And now Ethan was opening up to mom. He could now tell her things about his private life, things that would have sent dad into a worse rage. Serena already knew, of course, but she would listen anyhow and try to help her mom to understand this new world of alternative living arrangements.

Alex completed the long-awaited staff performance review meetings. The staff knew they were doing a great job. They all loved working for her. So the reviews turned into personal problem sessions after they disposed of the work part.

Alex was sensitive to the importance of keeping staff members happy, and work-life balance played a huge part. She was the voice of experience in that regard. She did not want her employees to give up their personal lives for the job. So she listened attentively to them.

Ethan had a boyfriend. In fact, he admitted to Alex that the Filipino job applicant, Logan, was his life partner. He was hoping that Alex would hire him because eventually they wanted to become business partners in a bookstore. It would be a great learning opportunity.

Alex said she would give it some thought. She wanted to run it by Ben. She didn't think it would be a problem. She had every confidence in Ethan. Having his partner on board might be like cloning him. That would be a good thing. Ben agreed. So she hired him.

Rishi's performance review was glowing too. Alex tried not to take him for granted. He was her loyal assistant. He was always there. Holding up the walls, as they say. He needed a raise and time off too. But he said he had no travel plans so he'd like to hold his vacation for the future.

Nobody knew anything about Rishi's private life. He never mentioned a special friend or even going out with the guys. He liked sports, movies, and books. Alex wouldn't pry. He was such a well-mannered shy young man, with nice clothes, suitable for a corporation, and glowing comments about his work. Customers loved him.

Alex thought he and his mom should buy a duplex together, maybe a house like Darlene's. He could have his own place and still be close to his mom. Of course, she couldn't or wouldn't even suggest such a thing, but it seemed obvious to her. Maybe Rishi would be a late bloomer.

Ellie was on the payroll these days earning twelve dollars an hour. She was fifteen and going into her sophomore year of high school. She wanted to continue working at least until after Christmas. Her buddy was a paid intern, learning the ropes too. They would decide about working in January. Alex didn't want her to miss out on school opportunities. School should come first.

Her friend's name was Careena, which Alex had a difficult time remembering because she went by Car and sometimes Otto or Auto. It was a lame joke, of course, but when someone said Otto would do it, Alex occasionally got confused. Sometimes Otto signed memos and messages as Tesla. It was all great fun for the staff. She was a good worker and got along well with everybody.

Alex also reviewed Karl, the postal worker. They were right. He did disappear. He never got the jokes, he didn't have much to say, but he worked very hard keeping the bookshelves in good alpha order. He was always lurking around the back shelves. Hiding. Customers had a hard time understanding him because he was so soft-spoken.

Alex had the staff all figured out until Ben pointed out that she could very likely lose all her female staff at the same time. What if Serena decided to stay home with the baby? What if Ellie and Tesla both quit on her for extracurricular activities? It could happen.

Crap. And Alex didn't like Karl. She hoped he would up and quit one of these days. If she lost the girls and Karl, that would hurt. She needed to think about hiring. Better do it soon.

Next, it was Ben's turn. He needed to talk to her too. Maybe they could do it over candlelight and wine. She realized they had several things to discuss over wine, so they chose an evening and found a place in Cannon Beach that sounded nice. Also expensive. Ben was paying.

It was lovely, and the delicious aroma of excellent food wafted into the parking lot. There was soft music, low lights, and waiters in black. Walking in made them both wonder why they didn't do this more often.

Ben obviously had something on his mind. She could tell. He looked like he was rehearsing a speech to be given at a solemn occasion. They were seated by the fireplace. It felt good, even in June. Drinks were served.

"Okay, spill it, Ben. I can tell something's eating at you. You've got that worried-professor look."

"It's that obvious? Huh. I thought I was going to surprise you."

"Actually, I don't have a clue, but something's up."

"Yes, something is up. I've gotten a job offer."

Alex was puzzled. "I didn't know you were

looking for work. You already have a job."

"Here's the deal. I've been offered a job with the Seaside Police Department."

"Really?"

"Yes, the Chief of Police job. The job every cop wants. The Chief told me he wants to retire. So does the Assistant Chief. There is nobody in the wings. The City is disappointed that both heads want to step down. The offer is to take the assistant job for six months and then move to Chief. They will hire a new assistant when I move up unless I like somebody in the ranks."

"Well, that's interesting. I take it that it appeals to you. Otherwise, you'd have turned it down."

"Yes. That's exactly it. I'd love to be back on the job again. I never considered the Seaside police might want me. A small town chief. It wouldn't be difficult. Not much happens. Not like the LAPD."

"So you'd like me to weigh in on your decision?"

"Something like that. I know you count on me working at the store. I can still talk to you about bookstore stuff and, of course, remain half owner, but as police chief, I'd probably have to resign as a bookseller behind a cash register."

Alex smiled. "And the police chief job would pay better too."

"Ha ha. Yes, it's not a great salary, but better than what I get now."

Alex said, "I can't think of a reason why you shouldn't say yes. It's a lovely offer. And it would suit you. I'd have to replace you, of course. I know you do a ton of work around the store."

He said, "There are things I can do, behind-the-scenes work. Running the cash register, probably not."

"So, is police chief a dangerous job?"

"This is a quiet town most of the time. I don't think the chief has to go out on dangerous runs. But it depends. In Copland, you never know. Big city chiefs never leave their desks. I'd probably be more active than that. Cops have to fill the shifts. I imagine the town police are stretched pretty thin.

"Most small-town problems are with domestic disputes, like the Serena deal. That was huge for the cops. They had to shoot somebody.

"It's like a bookstore. Sometimes you are short-handed. Then it's all hands."

Alex could tell he was excited about it. Why not? He had to resign too soon from his last cop job. This might be the perfect thing for him. Put his cop skills to use again.

"So, congratulations. When do you start?"

Ben grinned. "I'm not sure. I told them I'd think about it. I guess I'm done thinking. So maybe I'll be on the job fairly soon."

The entrees showed up. They each ordered steak. It hit their plates, still sizzling. The potatoes were perfectly baked. A fitting meal for the new chief of police.

Then the other pending topic. Ben broached it. Wasn't it time that they got married? Yes, it was. Should they do a bookstore wedding or a beach wedding?

"Hmm," said Alex, "maybe it would be fun to get married at the bookstore."

They laughed about it. Not many invitations to send out. Neither of them had kept track of past friends. Maybe a few stray relatives would show up. Alex loved the cupcakes and champagne idea. They decided to check with Serena about an opening in the wedding schedule. Another inside joke.

Later that night, after their date night dinner, Alex was reviewing the employee situation. By January, Ben would be gone from his bookstore gig. And she might lose the three women, and Karl, the postal worker, might be receiving his exit interview. That would leave her, Ethan, Logan, and Rishi to run the store, an impossible situation.

For one thing, Serena's event planning and computer skills were superb and nearly irreplaceable. Could she find that combination in the next employee? Ellie's compulsive ability to get used books ready for the shelves made a huge difference in the way the store looked. It was tedious work. Who would do it?

She and Ethan would take over book scouting and estate previews. Ben was good at prowling around looking for stock. She would miss that helpful duty.

So she would put up a 'Help Wanted' sign and see what developed. She also needed to have a meeting with her accountant. The meetings seemed unending.

Outwardly, the bookstore looked prosperous. Several weddings were booked. Other parties had been suggested. Serena was working on them. There was plenty of inventory to put out. Interesting window displays were in the works.

Alex worked hard in the background keeping all the ducks in a row. There were so many details about running a bookstore that weren't obvious. She was constantly multitasking. When she was needed on the floor or behind the cash register, she usually reminded herself of the phone calls and emails that were waiting. Something was always pending, and truth be told, it wasn't all that fun. No part of running the store was much fun.

She would tell nobody about that. Her old job wasn't much fun either, so she didn't yearn for it. A person has to do something with their life. She just hadn't found work that suited her. Something that she couldn't wait to do the next day. What could that be?

Ben and Alex scheduled the wedding for the next available date. Two weeks away. Serena and the staff took care of all the details. There was a very short guest list. Books were not needed as gifts. They also didn't need to go off on a honeymoon. Ben had started his new job so he was barely paying attention.

The interesting group of people attending the ceremony included Ben's new bosses and their wives, Serena's husband Jamar, Ethan's mom, Darlene and Tru, and the staff, with any plus ones they chose. It was a small enough group to have a catered sit-down dinner, which was delicious. Thanks to Jamar's connections.

The big hit gift was a bookstore cat. Serena went to the pound and talked to various rescue agencies, looking for the perfect candidate. They found a three-year-old with the proper resume. He came with a staff guarantee that he would be looked after properly. It was evident that the cat, a friendly, self-confident orange tabby named Steve, loved Ben and books.

The guests were in on it, so all gifts were cat-related. They got beds, toys, blankies, cat food, cat treats, scratching posts, and the latest high-end litter box. The cops gave a nice check to the humane society in Ben and Alex's name. The wedding was a huge success. Lots of laughs and good cheer for the happy couple. Alex and Ben Derby were now officially husband and wife. And parents to yet another cat, Steve.

Ben's transition from bookstore clerk to Seaside's new assistant chief of police went smoothly too. Very private, hush phone calls and virtual meetings between the LAPD's Human Resources department and Seaside smoothed out the hiring process. Seaside's decision to offer Ben the job had been golden. They were getting a great cop. There would be no mention of Ben's previous LA experience in Seaside. To residents, Ben was the cool-headed bookstore owner who had single-handedly defused the militia standoff. That was recommendation enough.

The department was impressed by Ben's quick memory and interest in every aspect of how things were run. He memorized all the officers' names immediately. He had read all their bios and records. He knew who the stars were, and yes, there were a couple of assholes. He figured that out on his own.

Ben liked the chief, and he heard as a side note that the boss was suffering from prostate cancer and was hoping to leave as soon as possible. The mayor and city council were also pleased with Ben. Lucky to have found him. They wouldn't need to poach a good cop from a neighboring department after all.

Ben was in good physical shape. He had been moving around and lifting heavy objects, keeping in shape. He passed target practice and driving ability. They had uniforms that fit him until Ben could get some tailored. Ben was a cop, it was apparent. He had a good work ethic and respected the force. Everybody was happy.

He read the cases and listened intently to the stories about the problems. He made the rounds of neighboring departments and met with the chiefs. He got up to speed on local cop politics. Figured out who he could count on and who he couldn't.

He also caught onto where Seaside fell in the competence rankings and what needed to be improved. He learned about budget problems, the hiring process, and the state of their equipment, cars, and buildings. Even the relationships with local government and prominent local residents were reviewed. He knew who the usual suspects were and who was untouchable.

He read the penal code at night to refresh his memory. And the local regulations, what to enforce, what to ignore, for now.

A person cannot step into this job and do it properly from the start. Ben knew that. He was doing his homework. He kept a notebook filled with his first impressions and his gut instincts. He would refer to his private notes often during his first months on the job.

Then it was time for Ben to take over. He was ready. His assistant would stay on for a while. They would partner on the big job until Ben was ready to solo, making it a seamless transition. Ben wanted to replace him when he was ready to go with somebody from the ranks. That would shake up the whole department. He had to make the right choices. His first political hurdle. He wanted it to go as smoothly as possible.

Alex noticed the subtle changes in Ben as his cop confidence emerged. She was okay with it. He was still a good guy. She could tell he was in his element now, doing what he loved. She was envious.

CHAPTER 19

July 4th is a police headache. This would be Ben's first year as chief during this nail-biting night. With such a small force, it was difficult to be everywhere, and that's what was needed. Frustrated neighbors were pissed off at shitty creeps sneaking around trying to scare the daylights out of law-abiding, firecracker haters. 911 calls tied up the lines, mostly reporting illegal fireworks, and parties that were getting out of hand. Additionally, the big Chamber of Commerce light show at 10 pm drew big crowds.

The cops had a plan, the same plan they used every year. As many prowl cars as possible dashing here and there. Reserve officers and rental cops at the show, traffic managers.

Some cops had to be held back for the next day's bailouts and bookings. It was always an expensive nightmare, no matter how much planning they did. It was a great overtime night for all the cops.

Ben was the chief, but his assistant ran the show, made the spur-of-the-moment decisions, and hoped for the best. By three am, things were settling down. And the worst was over.

Ben was thinking that being a homicide-narcotics detective was much easier than this particular Independence Day horror show. But it was just one night, and they got through it.

They got lucky. Lots of gunshots called in, but no bodies. No hit and runs, no wives with broken noses, the kids made it home, as far as they knew. And no house fires were reported. More than the usual number of drunks, and several car accidents to deal with.

The hospital reported burn injuries and a couple of missing thumbs. No gunshot wounds, no broken heads. A few fractured arms, several overdoses, and a bunch of folks got hold of some bad potato salad.

Ben was in bed by four and back on the job by nine. Things would be closer to normal the next day. Alex stayed home with the cats, who spent most of the night under the bed. Even Steve wanted into the loft. He usually preferred to stalk the store and sleep on the books at night. Not on the fourth. He was under the couch.

Alex was on the couch, swearing at the alarming level of noise. She couldn't sleep, read, or even get involved in a tv show. She couldn't call anyone to commiserate. They were all just enduring the yearly insanity of too much booze, too many noisy firecrackers, and bad attitudes. Jerks pretending to be patriots.

July also meant that it was now high tourist season all along the coast. Seaside was inundated with visitors because of its famous Promenade, simply called The Prom by the locals, a long beach walk, and a town filled with shops, great eats, and old-timey things to do.

So Seaside Books went all out to deliver beach reads, mysteries, thrillers, essential and fascinating histories of the area, and a big sidewalk sale of all things beach-related that a Bookstore could think up. One bookseller had to man the outdoor sale and usually kept quite busy.

Starbucks now provided outside seating because the weather finally remembered it was summertime. The diner's menu changed: more crab and Asian salads, fish and chips, and in a moment of Oregon humor, they added gas station sushi, which sold out every day because it was pretty good. They too put tables outside with colorful umbrellas. Nothing says summer quite the way a beach umbrella does.

So the crowds showed up. And everybody was enjoying the interlude. It's possible to get sunburned on Oregon beaches despite the sarcasm of the deeply disturbed. The walk out to the waves at low tide could be a long slog. The water is always very cold, so thirst and hunger set in. The three businesses at the deep end of Broadway were there for them.

Alex was pleased by the number of customers walking in and then going out with bookstore bags. They were grossing way over five hundred per day. Everybody was working at full speed. Both cash registers were in operation.

The 'Help Wanted' sign was still in the window. They were collecting applications. Alex was eyeing candidates. She would be needing a Serena replacement soon.

Turns out, upon further review, Serena was having twins. Two little girls appeared to be thriving. Serena was soon going to have to stay home. She and Jamar were rethinking their apartment situation. A ground-floor apartment had become available with an enclosed private patio that would be perfect for them. It had space for a garden, a table and chairs, and a little play space. The landlord said they could move in there without breaking their lease. It cost a bit more but it would suit them much better. A larger second bedroom was needed. This apartment had that. Also, because of the patio, they could have a pet.

They jumped at it. The landlord sent the cleaners and painters in, saw to some plumbing issues, and replaced appliances. It was going to be like a home for them. The landlord also had a talk with them about becoming the on-site managers. They would negotiate their rent for manager duties. He was going to be traveling, and he needed a reliable manager. This couple fit the bill. They said yes.

Jamar sat down with the landlord, and they decided exactly what managing the apartment house entailed. Once they came up with an acceptable list, the landlord realized he was asking a great deal from them. Collecting the rent was bookkeeping. Most tenants sent it in directly to the landlord's account. So that was easy, except when they didn't pay. Then it was harder. They also would be in charge of getting repairs done, cleaning up vacant apartments, renting them, and keeping up the general maintenance of the place.

Jamar knew how to do this work, and he also knew how time-consuming it could be. Jamar and Serena talked about it. Could they fit that much work into their schedules? Serena had no idea how busy she would be with the twins. She thought she could make phone calls and keep track of the paperwork. Jamar would have to oversee the workers, do the inspections, and walk tenants through empty apartments.

They could do it but thought their rent should be cut in half. To about twelve hundred per month. That was what Serena made at the bookstore. So that was the proposal. The landlord accepted the deal. They moved their things to the first floor and took over managing the ten-unit building. The new place was even more suitable for them. They snagged a second crib, which went into the new bedroom easily.

Serena's mom worked up her courage and asked if she could rent their old apartment. She wanted to be close to the babies. Ethan had recently moved out of the family home. He and Logan were sharing a place close to the bookstore. Rishi could move in with her and take the second bedroom. Once she moved in, she could clean out the house and sell it.

It all sounded reasonable to Jamar and Serena, so the big move happened. Mom needed lots of help. The kids all had stuff in the house that needed sorting. They ended up doing a huge estate sale, much of it pretty junky, but they did their best to find everything a good home.

Serena and her mom went through every room and chose things for her apartment that meant the most to her mom. Some of it had never been used. The so-called good stuff. She had good stuff stored in every room. The two laughed, finding old wedding gifts that had no purpose left but were now called collectibles.

When they finished, mom had a lovely old-fashioned apartment filled with new old stuff, perfect for her, with lots of room to spare, and easy to clean and keep up. She and Rishi would be comfy there. And she could be on hand whenever Serena and the babies needed help.

Serena and Alex needed to talk. Alex wasn't looking forward to the meeting. It was like the first domino falling. She feared she was going to lose all of her great employees, one at a time, starting with Serena.

Serena, on the other hand, was trying to figure out how to keep at least part of her bookstore job. So they sat in Alex's little office with salads and bottled water and tried to work out an arrangement. Serena figured she could do website updates, and she could also do the event planning, the phone part. She could not promise to show up at the store for the actual celebrations. At least for the first six months, maybe longer. It depended on her mom. Taking care of two infants at the same time had to be very difficult. And she couldn't afford daycare for them. If there was any other computer work, she could do that.

Alex relaxed a little. At least she wasn't going to lose her completely. They could definitely use her computer skills. She would think about other technical work for her. They both left the meeting much relieved.

Alex looked through the applications. No candidate jumped out. She wasn't exactly sure who she wanted. It would be great if Rishi took on some of her duties. If he did that, she could look for a full-time bookseller. A full-time employee could take on a variety of duties.

The store opened at 11, but she liked a few employees to come in earlier to clean things up and shelve some books. That kind of work could not be overlooked. There had to be employees around to relieve staff for many reasons: bathroom breaks, coffee, lunch, and dinner breaks. Employees also needed PTO and vacations.

And Alex wanted time off. A lot of time off. She was weary of running a bookstore. Even one that seemed to be successful. She didn't know what she would do with more time off. Perhaps she could become a better housewife. Learn to cook decent meals, clean more efficiently, and take an interest in the loft. Maybe go to yoga classes, meet some gals, and make friends. Take a class.

Perhaps she was depressed. None of those things sounded very interesting either. She was tired all the time, irritated at all the work that she was doing, and she didn't have any ideas on how to change things. She couldn't think of anything fun to do. And she was envious of her husband for loving to go to work.

Ben liked his office and the constant bee hive of officers coming and going. Routine meetings started each shift, cops handing over the reins to the next group of officers heading out to keep things safe in Seaside.

Two officers requested a meeting with Ben. Groan. He knew what it was about. The two guys had a long-running beef, somehow related to the job. It got so bad that there was an unofficial workaround in place. The two were never assigned together. These things are common, but with a small-town force, it was bothersome. Ben knew that eventually he'd have to defuse it one way or the other.

So one of the participants showed up at Ben's office with a wingman. And a chip on his shoulder. He was pissed. Ben heard the story again. He'd heard it before. Something about saying one thing, doing another, putting a guy on the spot to cover for him. Typical cop stuff, sometimes noteworthy.

When he finished telling his side, Ben asked his wingman why he was there. Witness, was his answer. Ben explained that as far as he was concerned, both were good officers so he couldn't do much to solve their problem. The problem became the elephant in the room at times. Ben saw smirks, eye-rolling, and hand gestures. Ben would like it to stop.

He asked the officer, "Do you have a plan?"

The officer said, "Yeah, it's him or me. One of us

has to go."

Ben said, "That's not a decision I can make. Are you here to resign? The thing is I'm looking for a new assistant. I'd like to promote somebody from the ranks. I can't choose either of you because of this problem. Your resignation would make my job easier. One fewer to choose from. If you quit, then he goes back into the running."

"Jeez," the cop said. "You're no help."

Ben said, "It's up to you. We can start the paperwork now, or you can give it some time. If you decide to stay, then the workaround is lifted."

"Fuck this, where's the paperwork?"

Ben said, "I'll be sorry to see you go. You've done a good job." He handed him the resignation packet. "Get it back to me soon."

They left. Ben was pleased. One of them had to go. Ben didn't care which one. Now he'd have to keep an eye on the wingman. And he'd need a requisition for a replacement officer. Personnel matters were not his strong suit.

The front desk guy poked his head in. "Your wife is here."

Ben grinned. "Show her in."

Alex was all smiles. "I ducked out for a walk. Everything is fine at the store. Ya wanna grab a quick lunch."

"Yup, if you're buying. This is a pleasant surprise."

They headed out to a sandwich shop for Clubs. And a little sunshine under a colorful umbrella. Ben told her that things were slow, so he had decided to take a few days off. Was she interested in a little book scouting trip tomorrow? Yes!

They drove up to Astoria on a bright summer day. Ben told her about his personnel problem. He hated to lose an officer but these things happen. He just hoped it was the right one. He could tell from the moment the guy walked into his office there was no hope.

Then they moved to her personnel issues. They were both familiar with them. Probably something she'd have to live with. She was lucky to have found the Patel family. They were a good group. Working at a bookstore wasn't a career job but the Patels seemed to be the exception to the rule.

They sailed through several good thrift stores and were surprised at the books they found. Since Astoria had some fine bookstores, they thought they'd have slim pickings. Not so.

They stopped for a late lunch along the river. It had been a fun day. A load of books in the back made it feel like they were productive. And they had lots of laughs. It had been fun.

They had wine, and when the second glass showed up, Ben asked her the question he'd wanted to for a long time. He didn't exactly know how, so he just waded in.

"Alex, it's been obvious for a while that you aren't really happy. Can you tell me what's bothering you? Maybe we could work on it together."

Tears formed at the corners of her eyes. His question took her by surprise. She didn't think it showed.

"I have been down in the dumps for a while now. I'm not exactly sure, but I think it's the store. Selling books just doesn't make me happy." She tried a crooked smile. She couldn't pull it off.

"I've learned the business over this past year or so. And I keep asking, why did I think this was such a good idea? I seriously think I've done the wrong thing, thinking that a bookstore was a good idea."

Ben thought for several minutes before answering. It was essential to get it right. He wasn't quite sure if she had analyzed her problem correctly. Maybe it was just one thing about the business she disliked, something that they could fix.

Finally he said, "That surprises me. You are so good at it. You've turned an empty store into a thriving business. From the ground up. You even lost your partner, but you kept going. I've been amazed by you. It seemed to me to be your calling."

"That's what I keep telling myself," she admitted. "It appears that I have succeeded. I should be happy. But I'm not."

Ben looked carefully at her. "Could it be me? I know we have sort of an odd relationship here, and I do love you completely, and I admire you. But am I the right guy for you?"

"Oh, Ben, you are the sweetest guy I've ever known. You aren't the problem. I sincerely think it's the store. I'm just not cut out for it. The problem is that I can't figure out what would please me."

"God, that's a tough one. We better give it some thought. Can we do it together?"

"Maybe. I could use some help."

CHAPTER 20

One day an older man came into the bookstore asking if he could talk to the owner. Rishi showed him into Alex's office. He looked to be about 60 years old. His suit was well-tailored and looked like Savile Row. His accent was British. He presented his card. His name was Lattimore, of Lattimore and Associates, London. And he wanted to buy her bookstore. For a million dollars. He had a self-satisfied air about him. Like the Cheshire Cat after a fine meal.

He mentioned, in passing, that if she took his excellent offer, she could not open another bookstore in the Seaside area for five years. He didn't want to compete with her. In other words, she was a success.

She gave the card a long look. She liked the feel of the paper. The lettering. There was no other information on the card. It was a calling card, not a business card. She had never seen such a card before. Right out of Victorian times. As she recalled, it was during Queen Victoria's time that the robber barons gobbled up the less fortunate. And handed out calling cards.

Then she checked him out. He had a pleasant look, not exactly a smile, definitely not a frown. He knew he had taken her by complete surprise. He was waiting for the question.

"Why?" That's exactly what she said.

He answered. "We buy unique bookstores, like yours. It has exactly the look and feel that interests us. Your quick success impressed us. We want to take over now."

Alex told him she'd have to talk to her business partner and get back to him. She simply could not say yes immediately. But she did tell him that she might be interested.

He understood completely. They would be open to negotiation when the time came. With that, he handed her his business card with local information on it. He would be looking forward to hearing from her soon.

She handed him one of her cards. He gave it a quick look and said, "Until we meet again, Mrs. Derby."

She called Ben with the news. He said he'd be home as soon as possible. It was dinner time when Ben showed up. Alex had cooked up a real dinner. She had purchased an instant pot and was following a recipe. She made a chicken stew that smelled good. And she pulled a salad together and served it up on her pretty dishes. All ready for Ben. A first. He was pleased.

They sat at their kitchen table, poured some wine and tucked in. It was all so pleasant. A sample of life without the bookstore in it. Would that be better? Alex was asking herself that question. Could she become a loving housewife? Her doubts were sending out SOS messages. She was trying to ignore them.

So Ben said, "Tell me about this mysterious visitor you had today."

"That bastard," she said, describing him in a way she just now thought of. "He walks into my office like he already owns the store and says he wants to buy it for a million. Like that would impress me."

Ben smiled at her. It impressed the hell out of him.

"Not only would I lose my business, but I'd lose our home. I love this loft. I didn't realize just how much I love our life until he was sitting there in the little office with his offer. He was more than a little too smug."

"Yes, you're so right. I think loft condos are going for around 700k these days. A condo. Peew, condo fees, HOAs, all that. Plus, your bookstore would be gone. If we subtract the loft from the store, we are selling the store for three hundred. We each get a $150k cash out. Doesn't sound like a great deal to me."

Ben was becoming skeptical too.

Alex added, "And eight employees, if you count Steve and me, would be out of work. The nerve of that guy. So British, so self-confident. Why, I never.

"Oh, another thing, I can't start up another bookstore in the area for five years. Like I said, the bastard."

Ben was surprised. He thought she wanted out of the business. Now she was furious that somebody wanted her store. She was having a visceral reaction. Like someone was trying to steal something from her.

Ben thought the store was worth about 700k and another 700k for the loft. So he asked her a different question.

"What if Mr. Lattimore upped the offer, say to $1.5 million. Would you be more interested then?"

"Oh god, Ben. I just don't know. If I really want out of the business, that's probably exactly the right offer. That might even be tempting. Am I willing to part with the store for that price? A difficult question. That's for sure."

Ben, being a realist, figured there were very few folks in Seaside who would be interested in buying the bookstore. She was looking at her potential way out of the book business, and it wasn't sitting well with her.

He was confused by her, but charmed, as ever.

Now he also noticed, couldn't help but notice, her sudden interest in the loft. It had been tidied up. There was food on the table. He never complained. He had lived alone. He knew how it goes. So Alex's sudden domestic turn might be symbolic, or it might be something else. He would pay attention and do his part. He would go along, enthusiastically, with whatever she decided to do.

Alex tossed and turned that night. She got up and did the dishes and then cleaned up the kitchen quietly. Went to her laptop, fiddled around with her incoming email, and looked at the latest best sellers, the Ingram catalog, Publishers Weekly, things a bookstore owner does when she can't sleep. Never thinking that she could pick up a book and just read herself back to sleep.

Some stranger wanted to buy her business. She had slaved away, worried her butt off about that store, and her employees toiled day after day in that store, helping her make it work. They had customers, folks who took pleasure in stepping into their literary make-believe world for a few minutes now and then. Why would she consider selling it now?

Could he buy it even if she said no? Of course

not. Could he trick her into signing the papers? In the middle of the night, that seemed like a possibility. Would Ben jump at the chance and force her to sell it, sell their home? He pretty much lived in his office at the SPD these days. Did he care one way or the other?

No! Ben never tried to trick her. He always helped her, and he did the right thing without question. She remembered when he first started working at the bookstore. He seemed grateful for the job, like it was a lifesaver. He did everything. He even took turns cleaning the bathroom. Heavy lifting, moving books. She could never question Ben. He was on her side. Definitely.

Her thoughts, one after another, were crowding in on her. She wanted out. No, she didn't. She hated the bookstore! Where did that come from? Somebody was stealing something valuable from her! What was it? Nothing made sense. No, everything made sense.

The next morning, after getting a couple of hours of sleep, Alex was scared. Maybe she was cracking up. The stress and anxiety were getting to her. She never acknowledged it before. But these episodes of brain chaos, as she called them, were happening more often. She was always able to talk herself off the ledge and pull her thoughts back together. Get everything lined up again. But that British jerk totally flipped her lid.

As soon as Ben left for work, Alex sat down at her laptop and started looking for a therapist. She needed to talk to somebody soon. She thought she might be in crazyland. The British guy scared her that much.

She could see someone virtually. That suited her. She found some contacts, therapists who specialized in chronic anxiety. After an hour of trying to make a contact, she started receiving responses. Amazing. She responded back. Soon she was on the phone talking to therapists, trying to find one with an opening.

One therapist must have sensed her near panic and set up a face-to-face session immediately. They had to go through a lot of setup information, payments, and consents.

Then they talked. Alex began by telling her about her brain chaos. The therapist asked her a few questions and then listened sympathetically. This was a thing Alex had never talked to anybody about. Her sudden panicky self doubts, her mental anguish about things that she couldn't fix.

The therapist asked her about frequency. And if she could connect the chaos and anxiety to particular situations. She put Alex at ease about it. It was a coping mechanism. It sounded like Alex had a lot of stress in her life. Her brain was helping her, not working against her. She said things that helped Alex immediately.

They set up another appointment for three days later. Alex was supposed to remind herself to trust the trustworthy. Like her husband and her staff. Get some sleep. She admitted that she used melatonin occasionally. The therapist assured her that it wouldn't hurt her at all. Go ahead and take it. Try warm baths, aroma therapy, and let her thoughts run free in a safe space. Trust them. She had issues to work out. The therapist would be her trusted listener.

Alex felt so much better after one session. She wasn't crazy. She was coping. She knew it was normal to meet once a week with one's therapist. But she was going to connect again in three days. She was grateful for that. To be taken seriously meant everything to her.

She didn't tell Ben or the staff that she was seeing a therapist. She called Lattimore and told him she wasn't interested in selling her business. No, she wasn't interested in meeting to talk about a possible future deal. Yes, they could call her in a year, but no sooner.

Ben rested a bit easier. All of a sudden, the bookstore problem went away. Alex seemed to be okay again. She told him she had called the Brit and told him she wasn't interested in selling her business. She also seemed interested in her store again.

Alex met with her therapist a second time. There was so much to tell her. They began an extended conversation to unpack her frustration with her life in general. Alex recalled how nearly hysterical she became thinking that the British guy was going to take her bookstore away from her. It was like he would end up with it no matter what she did.

Her therapist asked her if anyone had ever taken something from her. At first Alex said no, not that she could recall. Then she went quiet. The therapist let her sit and think. She remembered that her workmates often took credit for her work. The boss would expect her to come up with ideas. He would claim them as his own and get rewarded for them. He told her to get over it. She was paid to come up with ideas.

She felt angry about it. Especially when there was a reward given. Even small rewards like Starbucks cards, a day off, and hundred dollar bills. Irritating. She stopped coming up with ideas, or she would propose lame things. She got laughs then, and her reviews started to lose their luster. She became a quiet quitter.

But she often felt like she had lost things, a friendship, for example. Lost love, several times. Her keys. Somebody stole her car once. But these things happen to everybody, right?

The therapist reminded her that knowing it

happens to others doesn't make the loss less painful. Right? Those were significant incidents. She hadn't forgotten then. The bookstore might be a huge loss to her too.

They talked about Ben. He found her. She just looked up, and there he was. It had been easy to fall in love with him. Others were not like that. She had had romances. Not successful, not long-lasting, not fun, by any means. She always felt like romance was running away from her.

That's what made Ben so special. Romance ran toward her. She would never do anything to jeopardize her relationship with Ben.

But what if romance ran toward her again?

It won't. Ben is once in a lifetime.

Has she told him that?

No.

Her therapist saw her twice a week or more often for a month or so. Alex had been in crisis mode when she called that first day. The therapist recognized her panicky voice and her sense of urgency. The therapist became her lifeline. The calm spot in the windstorm of emotions she was feeling.

Alex knew she was in trouble, but she couldn't understand why. The therapist gently directed the conversation and pointed out things along the way that Alex had never considered. Alex told her things that she never dreamed of saying out loud to anyone. It was helping her to say the words out loud. Hear the vibration of the sounds as she made them. The incidents, the hurts, the small successes that kept her going.

The breakthrough came when the therapist re-interpreted Alex's journey from Silicon Valley to Seaside. Alex's version was that it was a foolhardy, ill-advised attempt to fix something that didn't actually need fixing. She and Darlene probably would have been better off to just take the day off, have a great lunch and a spa treatment. And then go back to work.

Alex realized that they had made a big mistake when Darlene bailed out and was now back at work in Silicon Valley, remotely, doing the same job in worse weather.

The therapist told Alex that there was a different interpretation she might want to consider. It was called the hero's journey. Alex had finally become the hero in her own life's journey. She was no longer the unfortunate victim in somebody else's story.

Alex listened. This was news. A way of looking at life from a perspective she had never considered. Life is a series of obstacles. How you handle them is your path, your journey. Do you follow the hero's journey, or do you stray off the path and become a victim in some other hero's journey?

They analyzed Alex's Silicon Valley life. She was a well-educated, hard-working drone in a large, successful tech business. Her identification was a piece of plastic around her neck. She was tied day and night to a laptop and an iPhone doing somebody else's work. She had little time off the job. The men in her life were just like her, their passion for life subsumed into the work product. Her ideas were stolen from her. She gave up her childbearing years to a soulless corporation. When Alex heard that, all she could do was nod. She was the definition of the perfect victim.

Then one day, she decided to rebel. It was a combination of things that gave her the courage to make a change. She had saved a pot full of money. Instead of buying into all the trappings, she had lived simply and saved her money.

She had a partner in crime. They came up with an idea. Run away to a totally different place, open a business, and put their energy into their dream for a change. Yes! Alex remembered those conversations. Yes, she did. They were so excited about them. They made a plan and followed through with it. While their workmates looked on at them mystified. They couldn't believe them. She remembered how giddy they felt. Escape was possible.

Off they went, Alex and Darlene, out into the world. Out of the air-conditioned prison of the tech world. To a place of cold, fresh air, rain, and angry seas where folks have to watch their money very closely.

Alex and Darlene hadn't given much thought to their business plan, but they had investigated Seaside and knew it didn't have a bookstore. Oregon is known as a coffee-drinking, book-reading state. Darlene had visited Seaside and knew it was a tourist town. It was small with money coming in, tourist money, not venture capital start-up money. A whole different ball game.

They found their store, and the two bright, talented women bought it for cash, and went all in, like promising entrepreneurs must. Then Darlene got sidetracked. A whole new journey presented itself to her. She had one chance and little time, so she jumped at it. Darlene's journey took a different fork. Alex must forgive her. Alex nodded. Okay.

That left Alex alone, against great odds, because most small businesses fold before the first year ends. Alex knew about hard work. She instinctively knew that bookstores are different from tech start-ups. Used books were going to be the key to her success. Pennies, rather than dollars, would be the measuring stick. She also knew from experience that she should listen to her workers. Treat them well. They were more familiar with Oregon quirkiness. She could learn from them.

She had a vision, and she had many obstacles along the way, but she overcame them. Even when romance came running her way, she didn't let it sway her from her vision. The hero meets many stumbling blocks along the way. They aren't always dragons, sometimes they are as enticing as a chocolate eclair. The trick is knowing that you can have an eclair or two, and still stay on the hero's journey. And that's what Alex did.

The final temptation to throw it all away came in the form of an odd stumbling block, a British banker, who threw her for a loop. He did try to buy her success from her. Yes, he did. She almost went for it because she was weary. She had won the battle, but she didn't quite realize it. Until the British Cheshire cat showed up and teased her with a shiny object.

He wanted what was hers. And he nearly got it. Why? Because Alex didn't believe in herself quite enough. She hadn't stopped to think things through carefully.

Her acknowledgement came slowly, with the help of her therapist, who was also a romantic and a reader. She was the kind of therapist who could see what wasn't quite so obvious at first. Her job was to convince a strong bright woman that she had been on a quest, a hero's journey. And she had succeeded. No, she wasn't crazy at all. She was just worn out. She needed an objective stranger to help her see things from a fresh perspective.

It all made sense to Alex. Everything. For once in her life, everything made sense. She knew what was essential and what was simply a chocolate eclair. This kind therapist had literally saved her life. And Ben and her happiness, and most of all, the bookstore.

She also knew one other thing. The bookstore was a chocolate eclair at the moment. It was going to be her job to turn it into an institution. That honor would not belong to that British Cheshire Cat.

There was still more work to be done. Her hero's journey wasn't quite over yet.

CHAPTER 21

Alex tackled running the bookstore with renewed energy. Now she understood just what it meant to be a successful entrepreneur. She would not sell off that accomplishment to a British Cheshire Cat. She referred to it as the Lattimore incident. And that was only when she and Ben talked about it.

She credited her therapist for saving her from herself. She realized now that occasionally she was her own worst enemy. She needed somebody to warn her when those thoughts crept in.

The bookstore was like a young child. It needed care and guidance to become a Seaside institution. A reliable place to go for books and for a friendly face.

Alex had no intention to run the store for the rest of her life. She had a plan to turn it over to the Patel kids when the time came. She figured Ben would eventually tire of being chief of such a small-town police department. Maybe he would get a job offer in a bigger town. Would she go with him? In a hot minute she would. She would tell him that at their next candlelit dinner.

In the meantime she had work to do. It was time to do some hiring. She needed a Serena clone and a Ben clone but she would settle for the best of the lot among the applicants she had. She read through them. She didn't know their ages but she could tell the more mature candidates from the kids. There was also an essay test with their applications. The last question asked the applicant to explain, in a few words, why they wanted to work in a bookstore.

First she separated the pile by who answered the question from the ones who didn't. She then looked at the didn'ts and tossed most of them. For obvious reasons. Next she looked at the women. First at the older ones. Probably her best shot for a reliable long-term employee. She set aside four. Then she looked at the young women. None appealed to her. One said she was a friend of Ellie's but Ellie didn't know her.

Then she looked at the men. Best handwriting landed on top. That also correlated with age. She chose two. Then she handed off the chosen ones to Ethan to make appointments. She figured the next time she did this, Ethan would sit in with her. She'd like him to do the hiring in the future.

Candidates would start showing up soon. She texted Serena to see how she was doing. Any day, Serena answered. She was having a hard time getting around. She felt like a beached whale. Oof.

Then Alex texted Darlene. Same question.

Dar asked, "Could you come by for coffee?"

Alex looked around. Figured she could leave. She told Dar she was on her way.

Darlene was feeling okay. Her little girl could play now. A good thing. It gave her some breathing room. She was hoping to get out a little more. Maybe make some friends with other moms. She was worried about Tru again. Just when she thought things were going well, he'd do something stupid.

"What now?"

Dar wasn't sure. "He left two nights earlier and said he would be working overtime. Don't wait up. He never came home. No calls, no texts."

"How long has he been gone?"

"Two nights. And three days, I guess."

"Jeez, Dar. I think you should call the cops. He's a missing person."

Alex called Ben. He sent someone out immediately. Alex stayed to entertain the toddler while Dar talked to the cops.

They came and made notes. Got a photo. And Tru's phone number. Dar tried calling him again, but still no answer.

They would make some inquiries and get back

to her. The cops sat outside for a while. Making calls. Then they took off in a hurry.

Alex asked if Dar wanted her to stay. She said she was okay, but Alex could tell she wasn't. She made some coffee and they sat for a while and tried to make small talk. Dar became more upset as time went on. She should have called the cops earlier.

Alex tried to smooth things over. No matter what was going on, there was nothing she could have done about it.

Alex suggested she get dressed. Maybe take the little one downstairs to her caretaker. That way she could be ready to go if they needed her.

Okay.

Ben called Alex. They were checking local hospitals, and following up with his boss. Others were trying to track down his pickup. He would let her know if they found it. Patrol cars were given Tru's license and a description of his pickup.

An hour later a call came in from Manzanita. A pickup with the same description was located by the river. Been there a while. Had a ticket on it for illegal parking. Cops were combing the area.

Ben sent two cops down there to help with the search. Then he called Alex again. Stay with her. They might have some news soon.

When Darlene got out of the shower, Alex was on the phone with Ben. She could tell by the way Alex was gesturing that something was up. Alex turned and stared at her. White as a ghost, shaking.

"What? Alex? Tell me."

"The cops found him and his pickup. Down in Manzanita by the river. He's gone, Dar. His...his head was bashed in."

"Nooooo."

She moved over to the couch and slumped down onto it. Moaning, "Oh, no. Oh, no."

Alex sat beside her. There was nothing to be done. They just sat and let the tears fall. Alex was thinking of all the years they had been friends. Darlene had suffered more since she lived in Seaside than any other place. The heartache must be awful. She met the guy that she figured was her soulmate. They had a child together. She thought they were working things out. Now this.

Ben called. Alex left the couch and took it in another room. They had found Tru's phone too. It was close to the body. It wasn't locked. He was seeing somebody else that night, according to the texts. They would know more soon.

Ben was taking the lead since he was the best detective they had. Stay with Dar as long as possible. He would come by and talk with her soon.

Dar heard the call.

Alex told Dar that Ben was going to handle the case personally. He would come by to talk with her later in the afternoon. He was so sorry for her loss. This shouldn't happen to anyone. They would do their best to find out who did it.

Dar said thanks, but she didn't care about solving the case. Tru was gone. That's what hurt so much.

It got worse, of course. The cops found the woman's address. She lived off the beaten path in an unincorporated area out of Manzanita. She wasn't answering their calls.

Ben called the local cops and explained that they were going to check on a woman who might be involved in a killing. Several other departments joined them. It wasn't far. They approached the house in a caravan and stopped just outside the residence.

A gravel track led to a garage, which was open. A pickup was parked in the garage. The front door was also open. Not a good sign. It looked vacant. Nothing was moving, no dog barked, no kids, no mom at the door on this Wednesday afternoon.

Ben and the others huddled behind their cars. They were all wearing bulletproof vests. It was a pleasant afternoon, not cold or rainy. A few officers had taken up positions behind their vehicles with guns trained on the house. Others surveyed the nearby properties. No other houses were close.

An officer with a megaphone asked whoever was in the house to come out. No answer. Another officer called the owner's cell phone. Somebody thought he heard it. They all got very quiet and he called again. It seemed to be coming from the garage.

Two guys in full protective gear went over to the garage. The others kept guns drawn. The two officers got close and motioned for them to call the number again. They heard it clearly now. They crept into the garage.

The phone was on the floor. The pickup passenger-side door was slightly open. They looked inside. Then carefully stepped away and came back to the cars. Two bodies in the pickup. Both dead. Gun in sight. Gruesome.

The cops huddled again. Two other cops, also protected, volunteered to clear the house. Ben gave them the okay. The backup was in position. They went in through the front door. Looked around the living room. Then the kitchen. It was a mess. One bedroom looked like a crime scene. The house was vacant. All clear.

They all breathed easier. Ben needed help finding the crime scene folks. The closest crew was in

Astoria. They would be there as soon as possible. Couple hours max.

The local cops volunteered to stand by until the crime scene crew showed up. Ben left one officer with them, his most senior guy. Told him to pay close attention and call him if anything unusual happened.

The guy grinned. "Sure boss."

Ben gave him a look. Then smiled. "Oh, I get it. This whole deal is unusual, huh?"

"Well, yeah. I've never been on anything like this. I'll do my best."

"This one looks like double murder, suicide to me. No manhunt. We just gotta figure out who these folks were, and what the hell happened. Make sure nobody else is involved."

They all nodded, putting away guns, peeling off vests, and talking in low tones. This was big city stuff. Didn't happen around here all that often.

Ben speculated that Tru and the woman were in the bedroom. Got discovered by another guy, probably the husband. Don't know yet how Tru ended up downstream. Husband most likely killed them both, then himself. A real disaster. Shouldn't have happened, but it did.

The Tru body dump would need some explanation. He gave that assignment to the officer who stayed on to watch the crime scene guys. Tru's pickup was down at the river and so was his body. Two bodies were in the house where Tru was supposed to meet a woman.

"Have crime scene go over that area too. So tell them three separate crime scenes, the river, the bedroom and the truck in the garage."

Ben assigned two officers to tape off the area around Tru's pickup, and stay there until crime scene folks showed up. Tru's truck might tell them the story.

The cops shook hands. Glad it was over. They decided who would follow up on what. Make sure all families were notified. If anything at all didn't feel right, make a note. They need to be sure this case was contained at three bodies. Ben wanted SPD to make the calls informing the relatives. Okay by all.

With all bases covered, Ben was about to leave. Then he remembered how green his staff was. This was a learning opportunity. Leave another guy. The choice was made. Four Seaside cops would spend time at a murder scene. Priceless training.

Ben's driver dropped him at Darlene's house. Alex's car was still there so he had a ride back to the office.

Darlene was a mental and physical wreck when he showed up. Somebody had to interview her for the record. He would do his best not to make her feel any worse. When she found out what really happened, it would be harder on her. This was among the worst things a cop had to do.

Ben knew her only part in this ugly mess was reporting Tru missing. She might blame herself for not calling in his disappearance sooner. Ben figured he had been killed late that first night. It was still light outside until nearly ten, so he figured around midnight or after that.

Ben asked her easy questions. She replied with simple answers.

He asked her when she saw Tru last? She responded that it was Monday night. He had to go out, overtime, he called it. He changed out of his work clothes, tidied up, and said he'd see her in the morning. Don't wait up. He was in a good mood. He left around seven. That's the last she saw of him.

Were they married? No, they weren't married.

Did he live with her? Most of the time.

Had this happened before?

Yes. He lied to her often. He said he was going out of town on a job. Or he worked late. Or he was checking in on his kids. He had women on the side. She knew it. He wouldn't talk about it. But she knew it.

Did she know who they were? No.

What did she do Monday night after he left?

She played with her little girl, gave her a bath, and put her to bed. Went to bed early. Read for a while. Fell asleep after she checked to make sure her little one was sleeping. That's it.

So he wasn't home the next morning? No.

Was she worried? Yes. She tried calling him but he didn't answer.

That's all she did? Yes. It had happened before.

What happened before? He didn't come home when he said he would. And he didn't answer his phone.

Then today you got in touch with Alex?

"Right. I didn't know what to do. I'm not his wife. I can't be like checking up on him. I don't even know where he works.

 "Alex comes over. I tell her that Tru hasn't come home for a few days. She says I should report him as a missing person. Honestly, I never thought of that."

Ben has no more questions.

"Okay. I think that's all for now. I'm gonna talk to his ex. We have her info. One of you will probably need to make arrangements for him. Does he have living parents?"

"I don't know."

"Okay. I'll ask Pauline. I think that's her name."

Ben felt bad for Darlene. He could tell she was barely holding it together.

"We will have to talk about him again, I'm afraid. As I said earlier, I'm so sorry."

Alex asked her if her caretakers could come up now. She had to leave with Ben.

Dar nodded. They hugged goodbye.

Ben made a report when he got back to the office. His timeline on the case. Who he talked to, and what he learned. It would become part of the official report.

The whole sorry mess was revealed within a few days. Tru was killed in the bedroom, most likely the couple didn't hear the husband sneaking up on them. A heavy pottery vase was discovered on the floor next to the bed. Tru's body was thrown into the back of his truck, which they figured was parked next to the house. No evidence. Just speculation.

The woman's fingerprints were on the steering wheel, hair samples on the seat of Tru's truck. She must have driven the truck to the river. They figured her husband followed her. The body was dumped by the river, clumsy. No attempt to cover it. They drove back. They were parked in the garage. They probably argued. The husband knew his life was over. He shot her, then himself.

The cops interviewed the guys Tru worked with. He was likable, fun, he loved the women. Good worker but not reliable. Tru didn't give out names of women, except for Pauline and Darlene. He liked them a lot and talked about all his kids. Serial womanizer. They weren't surprised at all. But Tru would be missed.

They located Tru's mom out of state, living in Nevada. She cried when she heard the news. She was living in a trailer park outside of Reno. Couldn't afford burial expenses. She thanked them for letting her know. She didn't hear much from him. She was surprised about all his kids. She cried some more and thanked them again.

Darlene took care of the cremation. There was no service. No ashes needed. She signed off on disposal by the crematorium.

She went through her house and packed up his things. She was surprised at how little there was. It wasn't really his home. Maybe he was homeless. He was just drifting from one woman to the next. How odd. He didn't even own one book.

Darlene's life would never be the same. She cried, threw things, swore at him, blamed him, and spent weeks in misery. Then she started to remember how much she loved Tru and missed him. Different tears now. Tears of sorrow for her little girl who would never know her dad. Tears for herself.

She had found somebody, but it was the wrong guy. So she just had to learn how to live with that. And the memory of their tender moments together. Treasure those memories. Try to forget the rest.

Her big move to Seaside hadn't been a total bust. She had a child now, finally. She was a mom. She had a job to do. Raise her little girl to the best of her ability. She had other decisions to make. Should she stay in Seaside? Live in the same house? Or go back to Silicon Valley?

Darlene learned that Tru's mom was still alive. Her own parents were gone. Dad died of cancer, and mom was gone soon afterward. Dar thought she died of a broken heart, but officially, a stroke, they said.

So Ames did have a grandmother. A gram who lived in a trailer in Reno. Darlene gave that some thought. Did she want to make contact with her?

Then another thought. Ames had half brothers and sisters right in Seaside. Closer. Blood relatives. Tru talked about them occasionally. Pauline had finally stopped bitching about child support. Dar should not be unkind. She had four kids. How on earth did she do it?

Did Pauline feel the same way Dar did? They

definitely had something in common. Were they both mourning him for the same reason? Dar knew that Tru loved Pauline. Somehow it never bothered Dar to know that.

She was tempted to visit Pauline. She picked up Tru's phone. Looked at his contacts. Alpha by first name. She scrolled down through lots of names. Found 'Paul'. There was an address and a map with a dot. Paul was home.

She gathered up Ames, her blankie, her stuffed giraffe, some snacks, a bottle of juice, her purse, and both phones and got in the car. She remembered to text the caregivers. She'd be gone for a while.

Pauline's place was about a fifteen-minute drive. Dar pulled up to a well-maintained, craftsman-style cottage. Pretty flowers in bloom, roses, succulents, and lush grass. Somebody was a gardener. She sat and gawked. Neighbors saw her. Waved. She waved back.

She was eyeing the large front porch with the swing and the rocking chairs right out of a magazine. A woman opened the front door and started towards her car. It was definitely Pauline. Tall, a few pounds overweight. Hair pulled back, jeans, long shirt. It was too late to drive off, so Dar just sat there. Pauline came right up to her window. Dar had to start the car for it to roll down.

"Hello, Darlene. I've been wondering when you were gonna stop by."

"Hi, Pauline."

"So, are you coming in, or are you just gonna sit in your car and think about it?"

She stepped back as Darlene got out and went around to retrieve Ames, who cried until Dar gave her the giraffe. Pauline picked up the tote, and Dar picked up Ames.

The house was pretty inside too. In the middle of the living room was a pack-n-play with a toddler asleep in it. Beside it sat an older child playing with some blocks. Ames sat down, showed off her giraffe to her new friend, and started playing blocks too.

An older woman in a robe and slippers sat at the dining room table. She had a cup of coffee and a crossword puzzle beside her. She was watching Ames settling in.

Pauline said, "Mom, this is Darlene and her little girl Ames."

"Oh, hi. So Ames is playing with her half-sister. That's pretty cute."

Pauline built a new pot of coffee, glanced outside for a minute, and then the three women settled in to get to know each other. They would spend the rest of their lives together, laughing, crying, and sharing secrets. Paul and Dar became like sisters, with the wise grandma beside them. It was meant to be.

CHAPTER 22

A few days later Rishi texted Alex that this day was the start of interviews. The first candidate would arrive in an hour. Alex was there in time. It was a slow morning, so Alex asked Ethan to sit in on the interview with her. Ethan needed the experience. So did Rishi. He'd sit in on the second one.

The first two were women. Alex started with a brief rundown on how the store was run and what was expected of the employees. Then Alex asked specific questions so they could get to know the candidate. They were looking for some relevant work experience, but they were also trying to gauge how well the person would fit in with the group. And of course, what kind of an impression he or she would make on the customers.

The first interview went well. They spent about half an hour with her. When she left, they compared notes. She could work out.

The second interview didn't. The candidate interrupted Alex several times to clarify things. She wasn't sure about using a cash register. She only looked at Alex, never at Rishi. When she was told that Rishi was the assistant manager, she seemed uncomfortable. Alex cut the interview short and simply told her it didn't sound like the right job for her. She agreed and left. They looked at each other and giggled. That was a first.

The first male candidates showed up in the early afternoon. He was dressed way too casually. He had on khaki shorts and flip-flops. He kept glancing at his phone while Alex told him about the job. He had never held a retail job before. When asked who his favorite author was, he was dumbfounded. He didn't think he would need to know anything about books. He left early too.

These were the cream of the crop. Alex wondered if unemployed candidates were grabbing any interview they could to prove they were looking for work.

The next guy was older and wore slacks, a dress shirt, and a vest. He looked exactly right. He was patient and interested, seemed to have a good sense of humor, loved books, and the wages weren't a problem. Both Alex and Ethan were thrilled. They hired him on the spot. He would start in the morning. He stood, shook hands, and thanked them. He left happy.

Two more to go. She let the boys handle them. Good practice. They were a little nervous, but the candidates wouldn't notice. The first one seemed too young. The second one was a strong candidate.

They huddled with Alex.

She asked, "Did either of them have computer experience?"

Oops. They all forgot that question. They would train them and see how it went.

They hired them both and then brought all four on board together. The introductions went well. They figured out the hours they could work. Then they discussed work assignments. Two were interested in scouting and previews. They all wanted cash register hours. Two would help get books ready to shelve. One wanted to open the store. The older man would tackle book buying from the scouts. They would all get training in basic shelving and care of books.

The comped coffee breaks and dinners continued for the new hires. Alex thought it helped keep employees happy. Small perks made a big difference. She smiled at the size of her food bill. It was significant these days. But subsidizing employees' salaries with free food seemed to be working.

Ethan and Rishi both felt good about the hiring process now. They could handle it in the future. Ethan and Rishi had made great strides in taking the reins. She would start handing over other parts of the book business as well. She gave them her books on how to start a business. They were eager. The store was thriving.

A week later, a couple more Patels joined the community. Serena delivered the babies without major trauma. Jamar and her mom were at the hospital for the pacing and hand-wringing. Mom was doing fine. They were small, so they would be at the hospital until they put on a few pounds. They were hungry, so it wouldn't be long. Serena needed a few days too.

The texts flew. Everybody admired the photos. Names soon. Preliminary choices were Belinda and Tanya. For those wanting to get the little ones something, think practical. Newborn pampers, extra small onesies, and washable blankets. The word went out.

Ben and Alex had another candlelight dinner. Alex gave him the latest run down. The Patel boys were practically running the store. She told him her four new employees were off to a good start. They were fitting in well, showed up for work on time, dressed appropriately, and got along with everybody except the postal clerk. Maybe it was time for his exit interview.

"My first one, Ben."

"You need the experience, my dear. So did I." He was thinking back to the officer who came into his office with a wing man, who ended up exiting himself.

"Crap happens. Lives change."

Alex talked with Hank, and they both decided it was time for him to move on. He didn't seem to mind. In fact, he smiled when she gave him the news. She got the impression that he was ready to collect his unemployment. She was grateful he left without incident and took his dark cloud with him.

And then Ellie announced that she and Tesla were leaving. They wanted to spend more time at school. Alex understood and told her she always had a job waiting for her with Seaside Books.

Ellie grinned. "Thanks, Aunty Alex. You have been so good to me. I saved most of my allowance payments from you. My college fund. I'm thinking of applying to the University of Oregon. If I am successful, I'll be the first Patel to leave home for college. I won't forget this place, and I would love to come back when the time is right."

They hugged. Alex asked her to keep in touch.

Ethan enrolled in the accelerated online business program. He was handling both the job and school. It was rumored that Ethan and Logan now lived together and were doing well. Mom was coping with it.

Alex and Ben were pleased with her progress in

shifting store management to the boys. As they became more confident, Alex noticed her work load easing. The store was maintaining its goal of grossing seven hundred per day. The store events, parties and weddings went on as usual. The new employees were so helpful and engaged. They appreciated working in such a well-run store.

Then their conversation turned to Ben's work. He loved being a cop again, especially being the chief. But he'd be happier in a larger town. She said she would definitely be open to a move if he got an offer.

He smiled. He lit up, in fact.

"What? Don't tell me you've had an offer?"

Ben nodded and then sighed. He had several. Word had gotten out about him. The small-town chief who knew what he was doing. So far he had fended them off. He didn't think they would want to go inland, especially to a red state.

"Well, you got that right. I couldn't imagine that."

"So, what would appeal to you? Bellingham, Washington, maybe?"

"You're kidding!"

"Nope."

She thought about it for a moment. Another fork

in the road. His fork, but it could be hers too. She heard they like to read in Bellingham. And she had never been to that part of the country.

They made a quick trip to the Seattle area. Bellingham was a pretty college town. Neither Ben nor Alex had ever visited the area. It was confusing, congested, and watery. They stayed in a nice hotel, were treated well by the human resources folks, and learned more than they needed to know.

The scenery was lovely, the ferries were busy, the traffic was astonishing, and the crime rate was high. So was the standard of living. And it rained the whole time they were there.

It was an information-gathering interview. Ben had collected what he needed to know. HR held a rather cool session with him. They were all happy when the Derbys caught their Uber back to SeaTac and flew home.

Both Alex and Ben were relieved. Bellingham was absolutely wrong for them. It was a city of about a hundred thousand folks nestled into a high population area of about four million. Ben did not want to work that hard.

They were delighted to be back in their loft. The cats greeted them as cats do, but soon they were all friends again. The bookstore did fine while they were gone. Ethan had a few notes, but he was handling things well. Alex was pleased.

Bellingham had been a wake-up call. Seaside was a great place to live. Neither Alex nor Ben wanted big city life.

It wasn't all that long before Ben received another offer. This one had merit. And it was close by. Astoria's mayor called Ben one day and asked if they could meet for lunch. Astoria needed a police chief.

It was an interesting offer. Astoria was about twice the size of Seaside. It was less than a half-hour commute, and they had some thorny problems.

Ben liked the mayor. He had met him a few times. He seemed like a good guy, smarter than most bears. He had a good grip on his quirky city.

They were having fish and chips at an off-the-beaten-path restaurant just out of town. For privacy, of course. The food was great.

"Ben, this is a job offer, so I won't beat around the bush."

Ben nodded as the mayor continued. "You know my current chief. Hell of a good guy."

Ben nodded again. "I agree. That's why I'm so surprised. Why would you want to replace him?"

"Here's the thing. It's a doozy. Chief's doctor wants him to take it a little easier, but he's not ready to quit yet. He came up with the idea of switching jobs with you."

"Really?" Ben was amused. Astoria wasn't a big city. "Is there that much more work to do?"

The mayor gave Ben a serious look. "I don't often talk about crime in Astoria. So this is difficult for me. We are a safe city, but we cope with the usual stuff, too much drunk driving and the usual domestic crap, which we all hate. But lately we've had some more serious shit to deal with. Not much, so we keep it low-key, but we are worried. Some violent crime, drugs, something suspicious around the port, and alarming gun sales. Chief isn't sure he can handle it. And now the doctor is warning him."

Ben reacted slowly. Those things could shake up any city, but Ben wasn't especially worried. He knew some things, remedies, strategies. He'd seen so much with the LAPD. So he knew he could handle it, and he liked the job switch angle. Seaside was quiet most of the time. His mayor could probably be convinced to switch. It would definitely make it an easy move.

Ben told the mayor he'd think about it. He wanted to speak to his wife first. And then, if it were okay with her, he'd brooch the subject with the Seaside mayor. They finished their lunch and shook hands, vowing to be back in touch soon.

That evening he brought it up at dinner. Alex was surprised.

"Is that a thing? Switching police chiefs?"

"It's news to me. But it sort of makes sense. The Astoria chief wants an easier job, and I'd like a more interesting one. I'm betting there's a lot more intrigue there than here. That would suit me."

Alex couldn't believe what she was hearing. This was unexpected news, but it was almost too good to be true.

Ben continued. "We could move there or I could commute. I was thinking of a possible third option. Maybe we look for a second home. We might find an interesting retreat to check out."

"Oh, I like that idea. You know I'm game for whatever you'd like to do. We keep the loft, right? I do like it here. And I've decided that I like the book business these days. That smug Lattimore with the big check was my wake-up call. I've got too much into this place to hand it over to that Cheshire cat. Ethan is doing so well these days. I have confidence in him. I can hand him the reins temporarily when I need to."

Ben was relieved beyond measure. He didn't want her to sell the bookstore. It was such a jewel.

Alex continued. "Plus, I have some ideas. Now that I have a store manager, what's my own next move, right?" Alex smiled. It was her fork in the road this time.

Ben was puzzled. "You've got that look. What's going on?"

She grinned, "You are on the right track, Ben. That smug Lattimore gave me an idea. It's easy to buy a successful store with great employees and become even more successful. Then take the credit. That bastard."

Ben nodded, warming to the subject. "But..."

"Exactly," Alex continued, "But it's more challenging to buy a store that's floundering, and turn it around. I've had my eye on one in Astoria that I'm thinking about buying."

Her eyes were shining. She was bursting with ideas. Could she do it again? It was a charming old store with a good reputation, but the owner wanted out. Wasn't interested in books any longer, couldn't keep staff, she was ready to practically give it away. Alex couldn't wait to get her hands on it. She'd been holding off for the right moment to spring the idea on Ben.

"So what do you think?"

Ben gave it some thought. His wife just kept surprising him.

"I get it and I think it's a super idea. Buy a bookstore that's failing, turn it into a success using your expertise, and earn the right to claim the credit. That's brilliant. And I think you just might pull it off. You're gonna face some headwind. The book business is staggering right now. But you've bucked the trend with Seaside Books. So we are both looking for bigger fish to fry in Astoria. That's such an astounding coincidence."

Ben laughed, "Our goal. This month, Astoria, next month Warrenton. Look out Cannon Beach. We're gonna take over the world, one bookstore at a time."

Alex was amazed. "You mean you're gonna partner with me again?"

"Yes, of course. Why wouldn't I? We're in this together, right? You still need someone riding shotgun. That's me, babe."

Alex couldn't believe her luck. Ben was going to partner with her. She didn't have to fight him to take this chance. First, her dream was to own a bookstore. Now it was save a bookstore. Astoria Books had so much potential. She couldn't wait to get started.

And Ben would be making Astoria an even safer city. What could ever go wrong?

The next morning Alex stopped halfway down the stairs and took a good look at Seaside Books. She smelled the candle they burned next to the cash register, the Scent of a Bookstore. Someone was making coffee. The place was busy, customers were shopping, and the clerks were all working.

She had created a charming place for book lovers. The hard work was worth it. She suddenly realized that this odd business definitely called to her. This was exactly what brought her to Seaside in the first place. The bookstore dream came true.

There was a glow coming from the beautiful Victorian doors. But it wasn't about past glory days. It was now. Come in and join us. Let a book take you on a journey. The books were calling, pick me, pick me!

EPILOGUE

Ben became the Astoria Chief of Police. He put the mayor's fears to rest. Yes, there were problems but nothing that Astoria's competent police force couldn't handle.

Alex visited the Astoria bookstore again. This time she made an offer, which was accepted eagerly. Now she owned two stores with her mostly silent partner. She loved her work, that edgy feeling she got when she saw how desperate things were. It no longer frightened her.

She interviewed the staff, and hired the ones who weren't burned out. She paid them better and added comped coffee breaks at the coffee house next door. And lunches at the cafe down the street. She wanted a good relationship with her neighbors. They could work together to revive interest in their downtown location.

Rishi retrained the staff and instilled a more optimistic mindset. Meanwhile Alex was planning a physical revamp of the new store. It was musty and tired looking. They did a temporary partial closing and sold the old merchandise outside on large sales tables, while painters and carpenters worked on a new look. The store needed an event space, a clean bathroom, and everything else shined up. Alex wanted customers to be intrigued when they came back to Astoria Books.

Staff members learned how to work with book scouts who began bringing in bags of books for sale. Even Ben got into the act on his days off. He would shed his uniform and cop car, and once again became an unpaid staff member. He would take a bookseller on the road with him visiting thrift stores and estate sales. They were often successful. And several times they hit a semi precious jackpots of used gems.

When the store did a soft reopening, Alex was surprised at the eagerness of the returning customers. The store was inviting, and eager to show off its new look. It even smelled different.

Seaside Books did some marketing for Astoria. Parties were explained. Get married in a beautiful bookstore, have a birthday party, a small reunion, retiring? Astoria Books was eager for the party to start.

Serena could plan the events from home. Her mom was working out brilliantly with the twins. Ellie wondered if she could drop in and pick up a few hours when she could? Of course.

Everybody got involved. More customers were heading into downtown Astoria. So the other local businesses took note and freshened their stores too. The coffee house added tables and more food items. Outside dining with colorful umbrellas. Customers were lingering. The cafe added bookish food to their menu. That got some laughs. They renamed sandwiches after book characters, added omelets, interesting salads, and millennial favorites featuring kale and black beans. Fun came into fashion again.

Success agreed with Alex. She had done it again. She put people to work, revived a retail street in downtown Astoria. She created wealth, as they say.

But it actually wasn't the money, it was the scent of the store. The armchair adventure. It was what books stood for. Knowledge is power, of course, but books are more than that. They are mysterious, and they reside in unexpected places.

They teach us who we are and what we can become. They warn us about bad things, the evil out there, and what we can do about it. They become our friends, and keep us from becoming too lonely. They teach us how to become more careful of our planet. But most of all, they store the knowledge of the ages. It's there. Just walk in. Welcome to the bookstore.

ACKNOWLEDGEMENTS:

I am one of those people who love bookstores for all the usual reasons. They are the places where adventure begins. For me, all novels are journeys. They take me somewhere else. They introduce me to interesting characters and situations, and together we explore the worst to the best that life offers. I have worked in bookstores as a bookseller, not in a position of power by any means. A bookseller rarely gets a glimpse into the decision-making that goes into success in the book business.

I worked at B. Dalton for about a year. I helped close the store. The Valley Fair shopping center in San Jose was about to become a mall. B. Dalton was one of the last holdouts as the shopping center shut down around us. So I experienced the death of a bookstore. We sold off books, we commiserated with long-time customers, and we lamented the loss of the familiar. When the time came, we packed up the books. And one last thing. We took down the B. Dalton sign made up of three-foot tall, gold leaf letters. I was awarded the Dalton D, which I still cherish many years later.

I also worked at Barnes & Noble's big store in San Jose for a few years. And I enjoyed it immensely. I still wander through it occasionally. I love the way it smells.

So that's the insight I bring to my novel about bookstores. Essentially, I'm winging it. I never read a how-to book about bookstore ownership. I do own a collection of books, both fictional and non-fictional, about books and bookstores. I did use my memories of those stories as my guide.

What I do when I write any novel is to come up with some characters who interest me and put them in a familiar setting to begin the story. Seaside, Oregon, is familiar to me. I grew up in Portland and spent lots of time in Seaside. Seaside, the town, is real, but everything I write about Seaside is totally fictional. Totally!

To begin my novels, I describe where and how my characters live so the readers can picture their lives before all hell breaks loose. I do let the characters tell the story. I don't have an outline of what will happen to them. I don't know the end when I write the beginning. I do know the point I want to make. That's what guides us as I live and write their story.

In this novel I wanted to write about the importance and the romance of bookstores. That special feeling we get when we walk into one. And the influential role that books play in our lives.

I want to thank my daughters, Sheri and Karen, for their continuing commitment in helping me every step of the way. I couldn't get to the finish line without you. And of course, a huge thank you to my good friends who patiently listen to me. A special thank you to Rosemarie Delson and Rosemary Joy for our breakfasts, to Linda Brown for our epic phone calls, and to Allison for Fridays. Writing is a lonely business, but having friends who are eager to talk and laugh is priceless.

I can't say enough about Kindle Press. If you have the technical skills, you can self-publish with Kindle quickly and at absolutely no cost. I have a lot of stories to tell, and I'm too old to go through the traditional publishing routine. So Kindle is perfect for me. Thank you.

Printed in Great Britain
by Amazon

37206084R00182